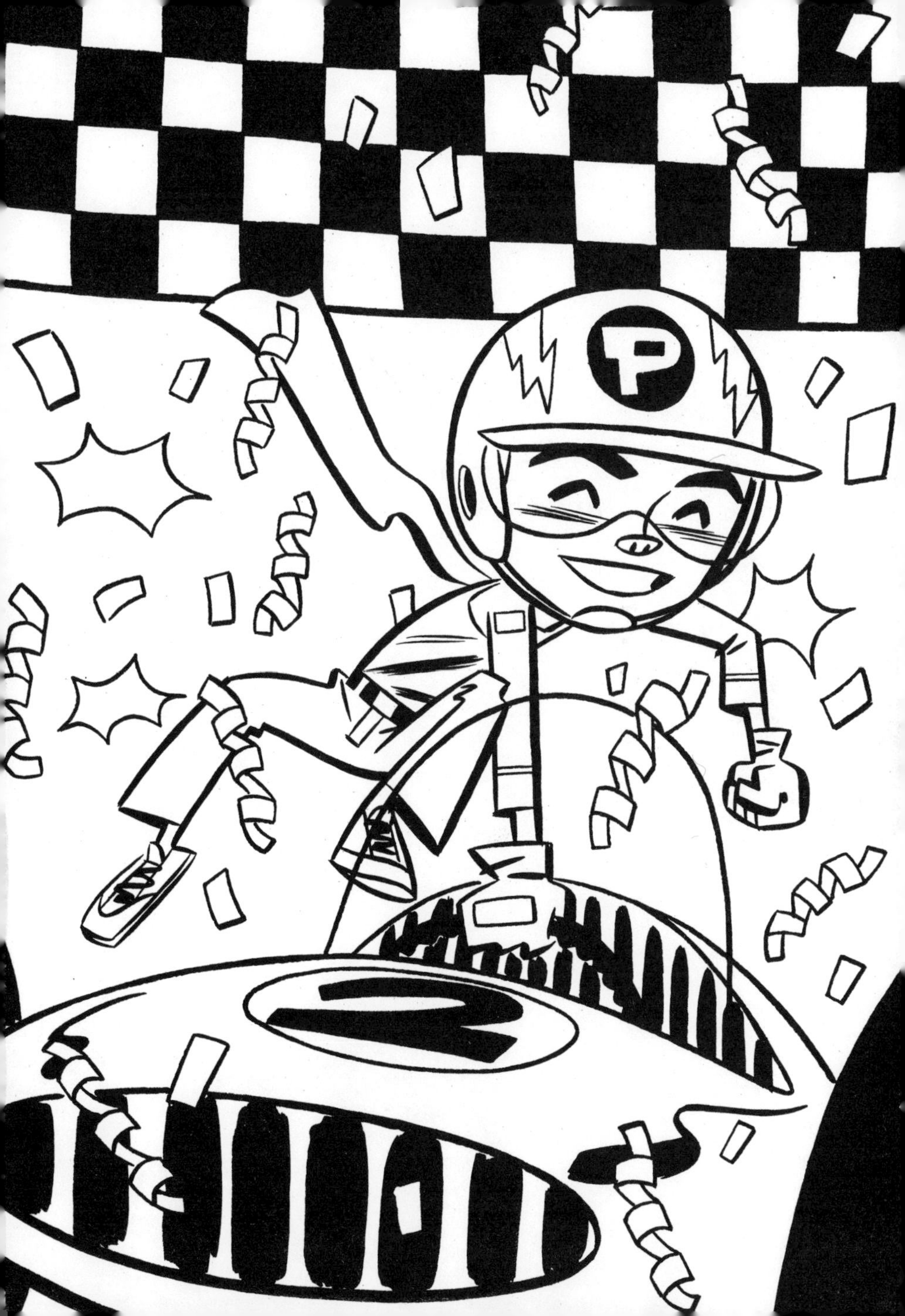

Also by Eric Wight:

Frankie Pickle
and the Closet of Doom

FRANKIE PICKLE™

AND THE PINE RUN 3000

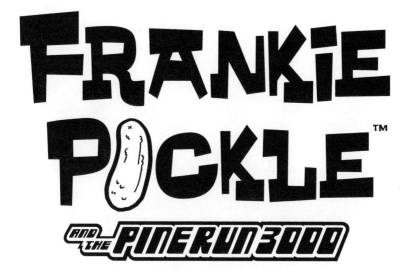

written and illustrated by
ERIC WIGHT

SIMON & SCHUSTER
BOOKS FOR YOUNG READERS
New York London Toronto Sydney

SIMON & SCHUSTER BOOKS FOR YOUNG READERS
An imprint of Simon & Schuster Children's Publishing Division
1230 Avenue of the Americas, New York, New York 10020
SIMON & SCHUSTER BOOKS FOR YOUNG READERS is a
trademark of Simon & Schuster, Inc.
For information about special discounts for bulk purchases,
please contact Simon & Schuster Special Sales
at 1-866-506-1949 or business@simonandschuster.com.
The Simon & Schuster Speakers Bureau can bring authors to
your live event. For more information or to book an event,
contact the Simon & Schuster Speakers Bureau at 1-866-248-3049
or visit our website at www.simonspeakers.com.
Book design by Eric Wight and Tom Daly
The text for this book is set in Farao.
The illustrations for this book are rendered digitally.
Manufactured in the United States of America
0215 FFG
8 10 9 7
Library of Congress Cataloging-in-Publication Data
Wight, Eric, 1974-
Frankie Pickle and the Pine Run 3000 / written and illustrated by Eric Wight.
p. cm.
Summary: Fourth-grader Frankie Piccolini's vivid imagination does not help him
advance in rank with the rest of his Possum Scout troop, but winning the
Pine Run 3000 model car race would give him the points he needs.
ISBN 978-1-4169-6485-8 (hardcover : alk. paper)
[1. Scouting (Youth activity)—Fiction. 2. Racing—Fiction. 3. Imagination—Fiction.
4. Family life—Fiction.] I. Title.
PZ7.W6392Frg 2010
[Fic]—dc22
2009015796
ISBN 978-1-4169-9880-8 (eBook)

To my dad,
who is always there to help—
even when I don't know how to ask

CHAPTER ONE

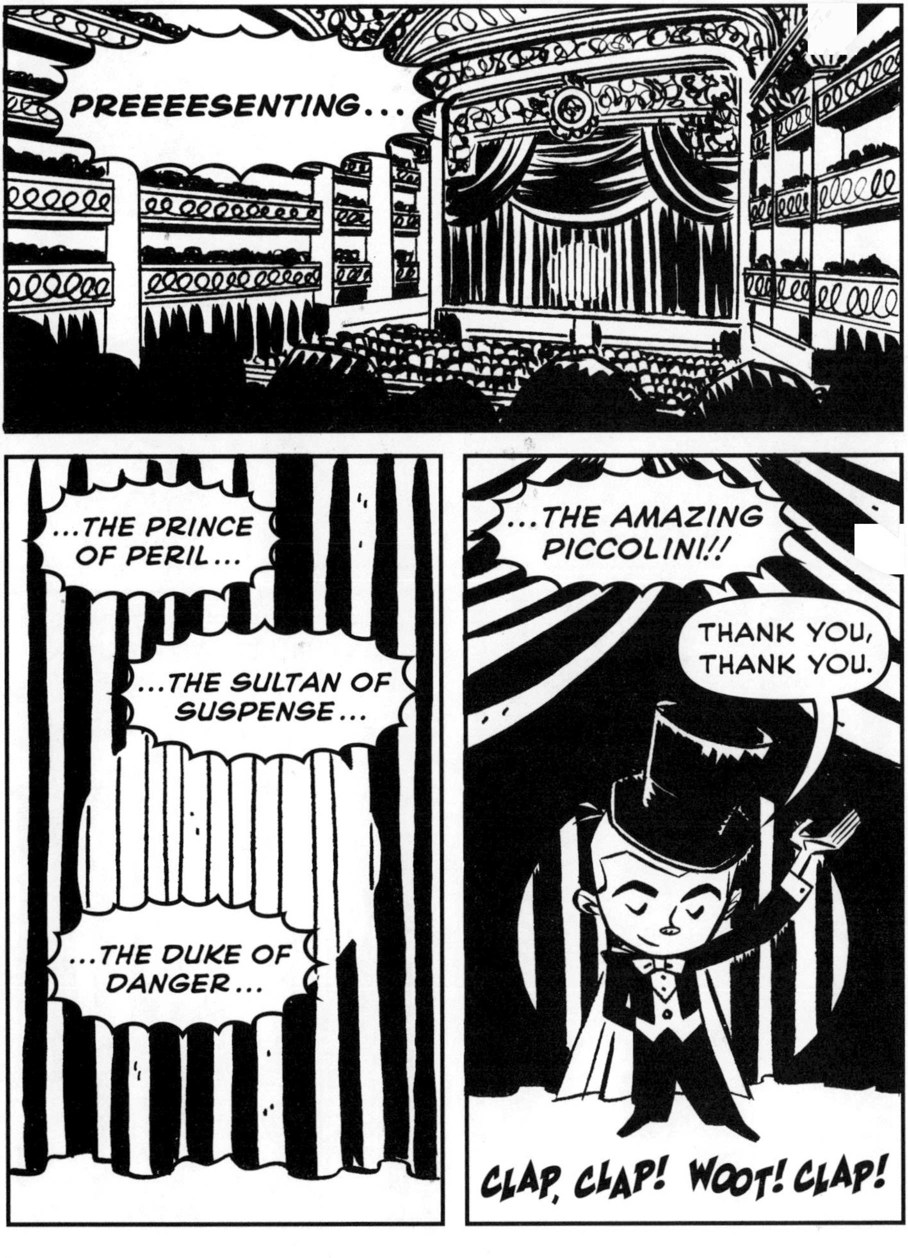
PREEEESENTING...
...THE PRINCE OF PERIL...
...THE SULTAN OF SUSPENSE...
...THE DUKE OF DANGER...
...THE AMAZING PICCOLINI!!
THANK YOU, THANK YOU.
CLAP, CLAP! WOOT! CLAP!

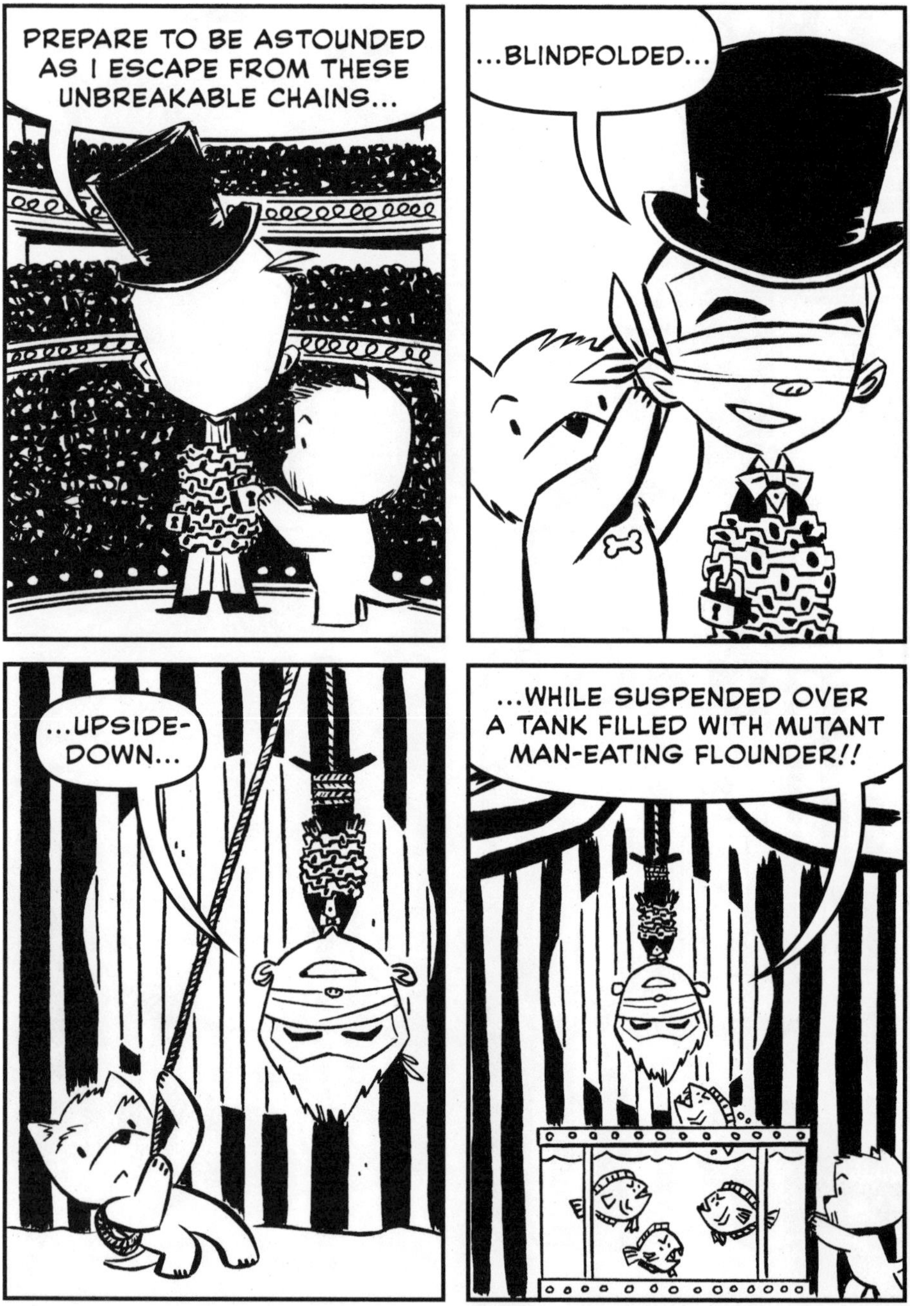
PREPARE TO BE ASTOUNDED AS I ESCAPE FROM THESE UNBREAKABLE CHAINS...
...BLINDFOLDED...
...UPSIDE-DOWN...
...WHILE SUSPENDED OVER A TANK FILLED WITH MUTANT MAN-EATING FLOUNDER!!

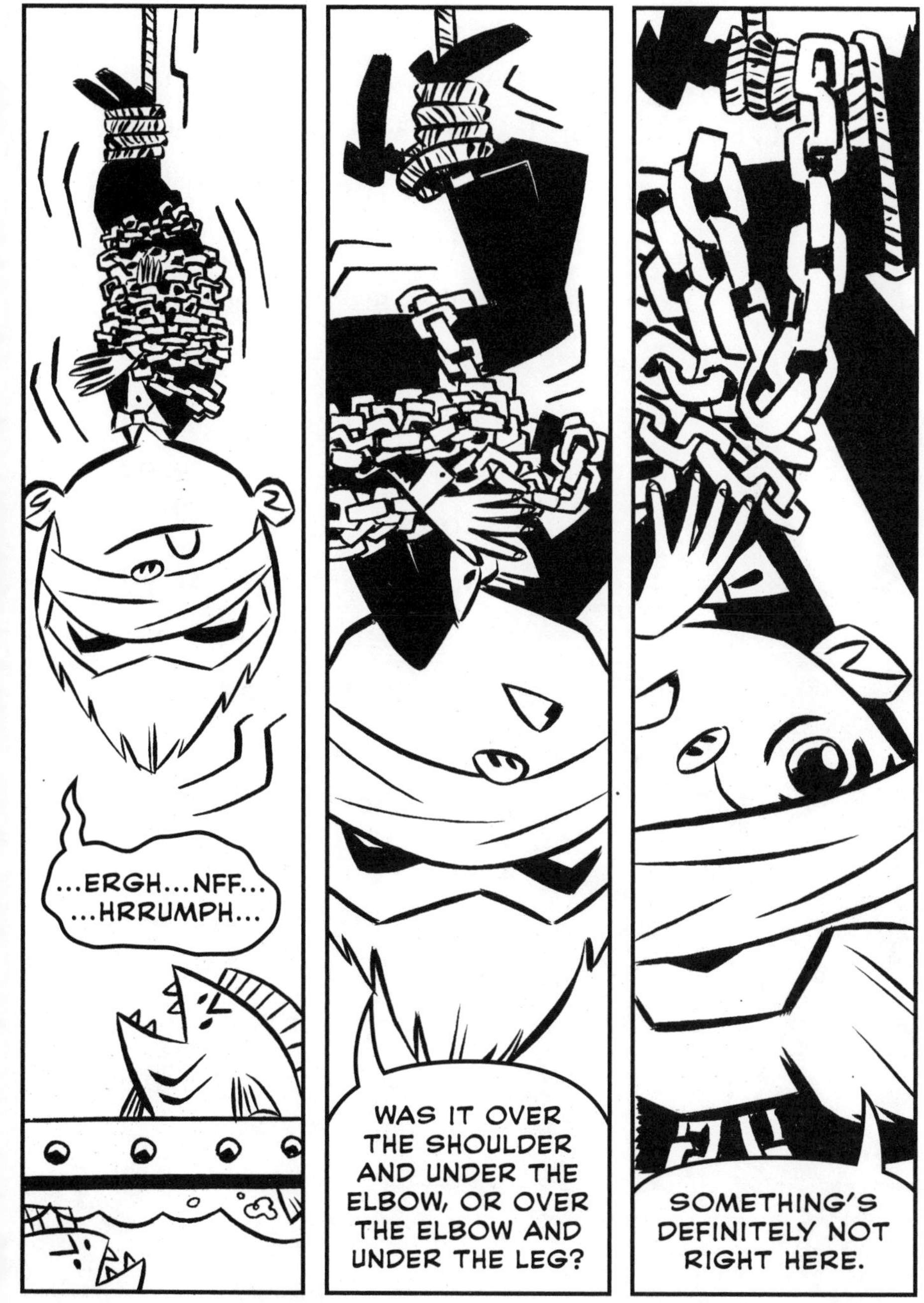
...ERGH...NFF... ...HRRUMPH...
WAS IT OVER THE SHOULDER AND UNDER THE ELBOW, OR OVER THE ELBOW AND UNDER THE LEG?
SOMETHING'S DEFINITELY NOT RIGHT HERE.

Tangled in twine, Frankie flopped onto his living room floor. He was too busy wiggling around to notice the stares of the other Possum Scouts.

"How did you get so twisted up?" said Frankie's mom, who was also the troop's Marsupial Mother. "You were only supposed to tie a basic sailor's loop."

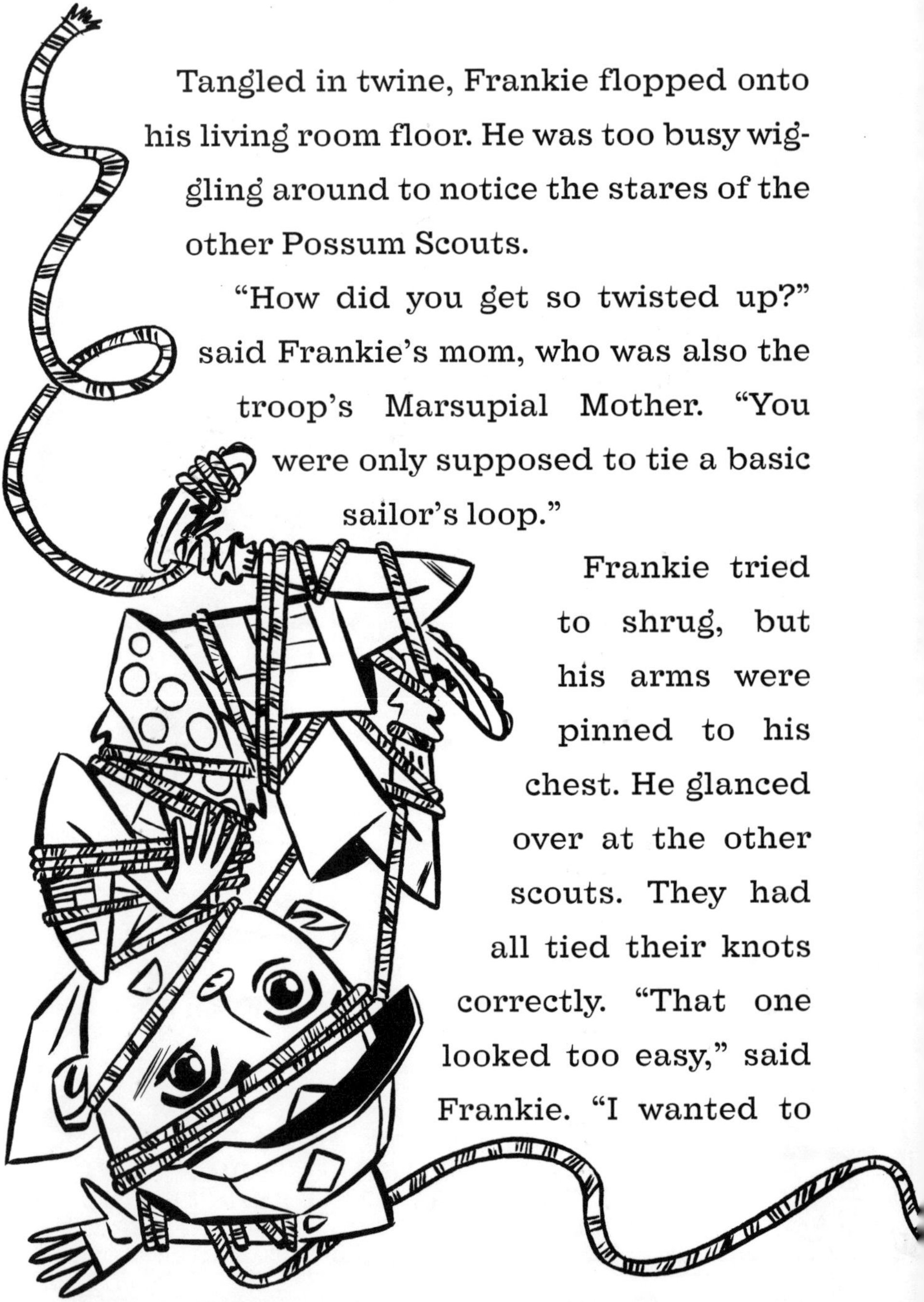

Frankie tried to shrug, but his arms were pinned to his chest. He glanced over at the other scouts. They had all tied their knots correctly. "That one looked too easy," said Frankie. "I wanted to

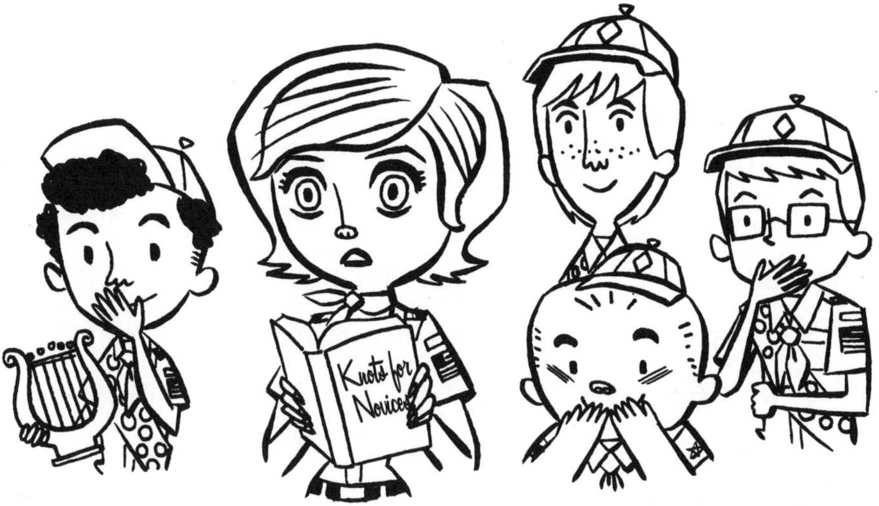
Knots for Novices

come up with a super-duper knot."

"Why didn't you just ask for help?" said Mom. She tugged at the rope. "This is way too tight to undo by hand."

"I get extra points for that, right?" said Frankie.

"Not when it's the wrong kind of knot."

The other scouts started to snicker. They'd probably be laughing their lungs out if Frankie's mom wasn't there. Even his best friend Kenny had a hard time keeping a straight face.

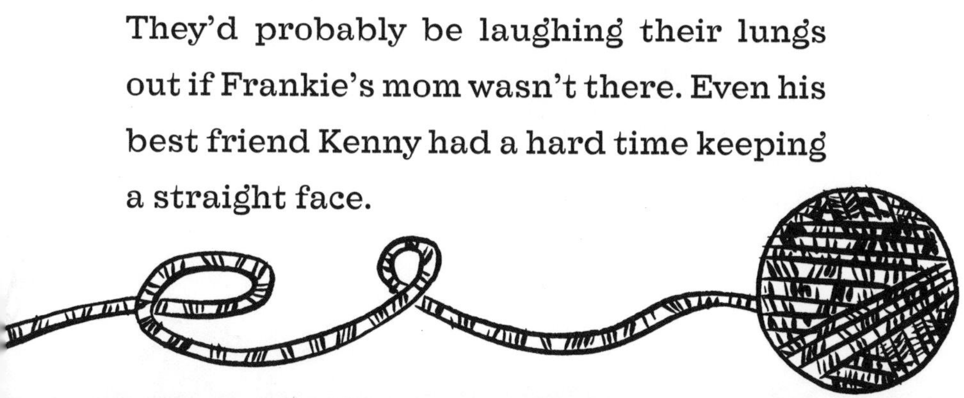

Frankie had to do something to impress them. "I know how to get free without any help." He sucked in as much air as he could, then tried with all of his strength to snap the ropes, like a superhero. That only made the knots tighter. The ropes burned his skin.

"Stop that before you pop something!" said Mom. "I need to cut you loose."

"Would you like to borrow my safety scissors?" said Carter Hawkins. "I always keep a pair in my emergency utility pouch."

"This ... isn't ... an emergency ... ," said Frankie, turning an odd shade of bluish-purple.

"Why, thank you, Carter," said Mom. "That's very handy of you."

"A Possum Scout is prepared for anything," said Carter.

And Carter always was. Like the time

when Kevin twisted his ankle and Carter made a splint out of Popsicle sticks. Or when Oliver got stung by a bee, Carter knew to put mud on the bee sting. And when Lucas got woozy from being hungry, Carter had an extra snack pack. He was such a scout super- star that some of the other kids were con- vinced he actually *was* part possum.

Carter unzipped the pouch around his waist and fetched the scissors for Frankie's mom. Then she went to work snipping Frankie's ropes—and pride—into little pieces.

CHAPTER TWO

After Frankie was finally untangled, it was time to hand out the merit badges. Everyone gathered on the living room floor around a fake campfire Mom had made from toilet paper tubes and orange tissue paper. Argyle, the troop's mascot, wore a yellow scarf for the occasion.

"This is a very special ceremony," said Mom. "Today marks the last meeting of the fall session. All of you who have completed the knot-tying badge have earned enough Possum Points to move up in rank from Pygmy to Shrew."

The boys all cheered. Moving up in rank was a big deal. It meant you now got to do stuff that was too dangerous for Pygmies, like shoot a bow and arrow, make fire, and go camping in the woods. It was like being inducted into the League of Awesome.

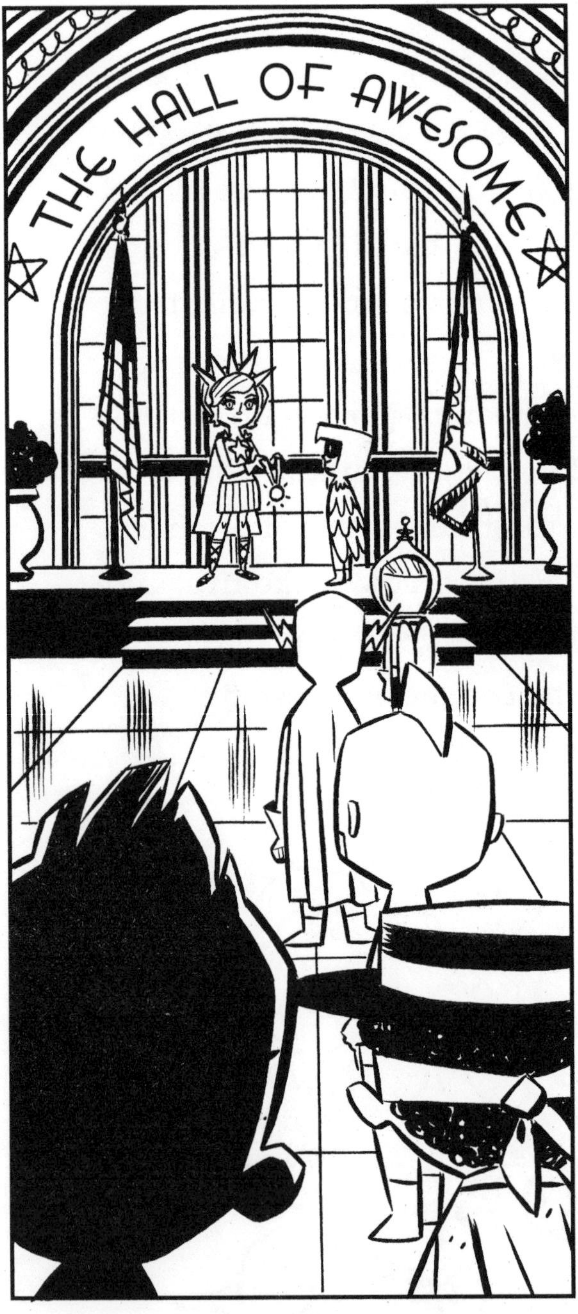
THE HALL OF AWESOME

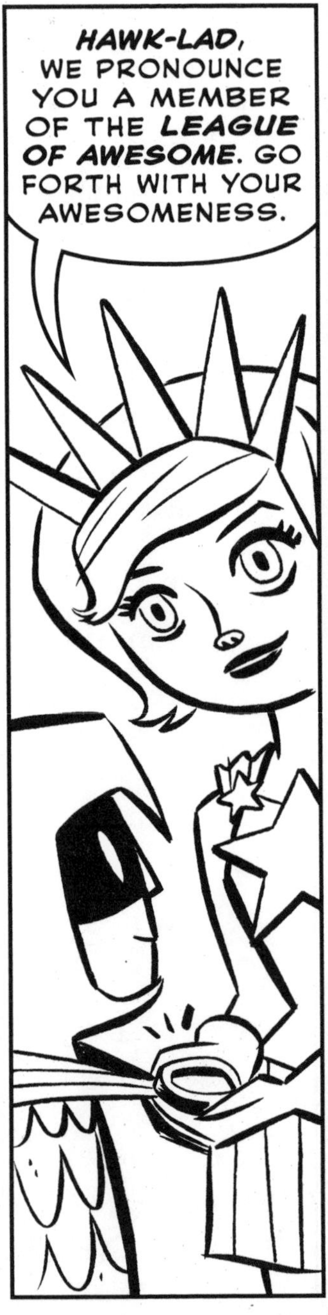
HAWK-LAD, WE PRONOUNCE YOU A MEMBER OF THE LEAGUE OF AWESOME. GO FORTH WITH YOUR AWESOMENESS.

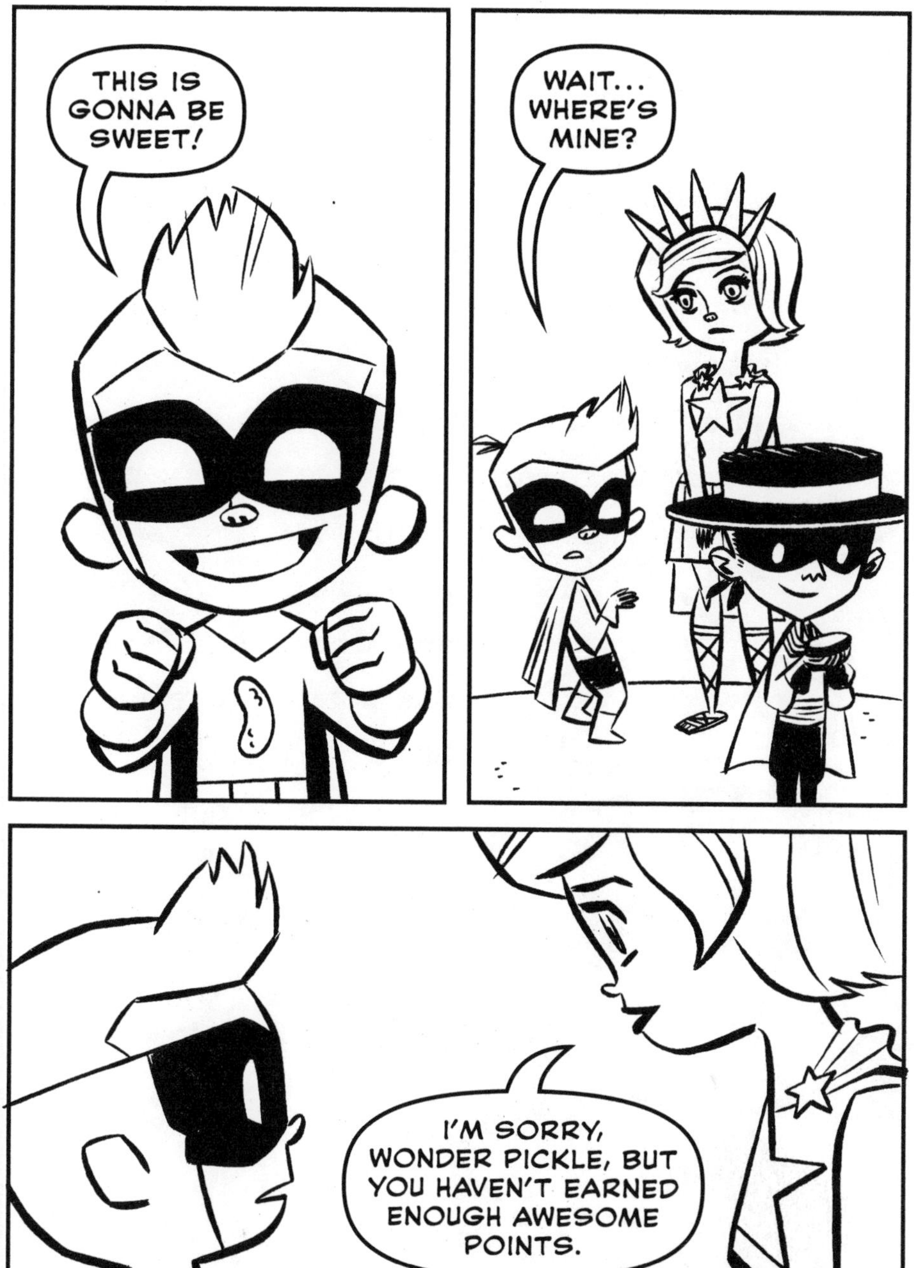
THIS IS GONNA BE SWEET!
WAIT... WHERE'S MINE?
I'M SORRY, WONDER PICKLE, BUT YOU HAVEN'T EARNED ENOUGH AWESOME POINTS.

There had to be some kind of mistake. How could Frankie not become a Shrew Scout with the rest of his Possum Troop?

"I'm sorry, Frankie," said Mom. "You didn't complete the knot assignment, so I can't award you the badge."

"But I'm your son," said Frankie.

"You have to earn it the same as everyone else," said Mom.

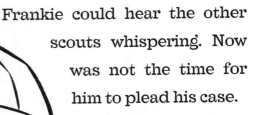

Frankie could hear the other scouts whispering. Now was not the time for him to plead his case.

"That's cool," he said. "I'll catch up with you guys at the next rank."

But truthfully, it was ANYTHING but cool.

CHAPTER THREE

Long after the other scouts went home, Frankie was still very upset. He went into the kitchen, where Mom was preparing dinner. His baby sister, Lucy, was playing on the floor with pots and pans.

"There has to be a way for me to move up in rank," said Frankie. "What if I do the knots again?"

Mom diced a tomato. "Badges have to be earned during troop meetings.

Otherwise it isn't fair to the other scouts. You can try again next session."

"But that's not for, like, a month!" said Frankie.

"I know you're disappointed, but those are the Possum Scout rules."

"THAT'S SO UNFAIR!"

Lucy banged a pot with a wooden spoon in agreement.

Frankie's dad and older sister, Piper, arrived home from softball practice in time to hear the commotion.

"What'd we miss?" said Dad.

As everyone sat down for dinner, Frankie brought Dad and Piper up to speed.

"Sounds like a tough break, Bud," said Dad.

"You're more of a weasel than a shrew, anyway," said Piper.

Mom gave Piper The Look. The one that turns people to stone.

"What about the Pine Run 3000?" said Dad.

"Of course!" said Frankie.

"What's the Pine Run 3000?" said Piper.

"Only the greatest race ever invented," said Frankie.

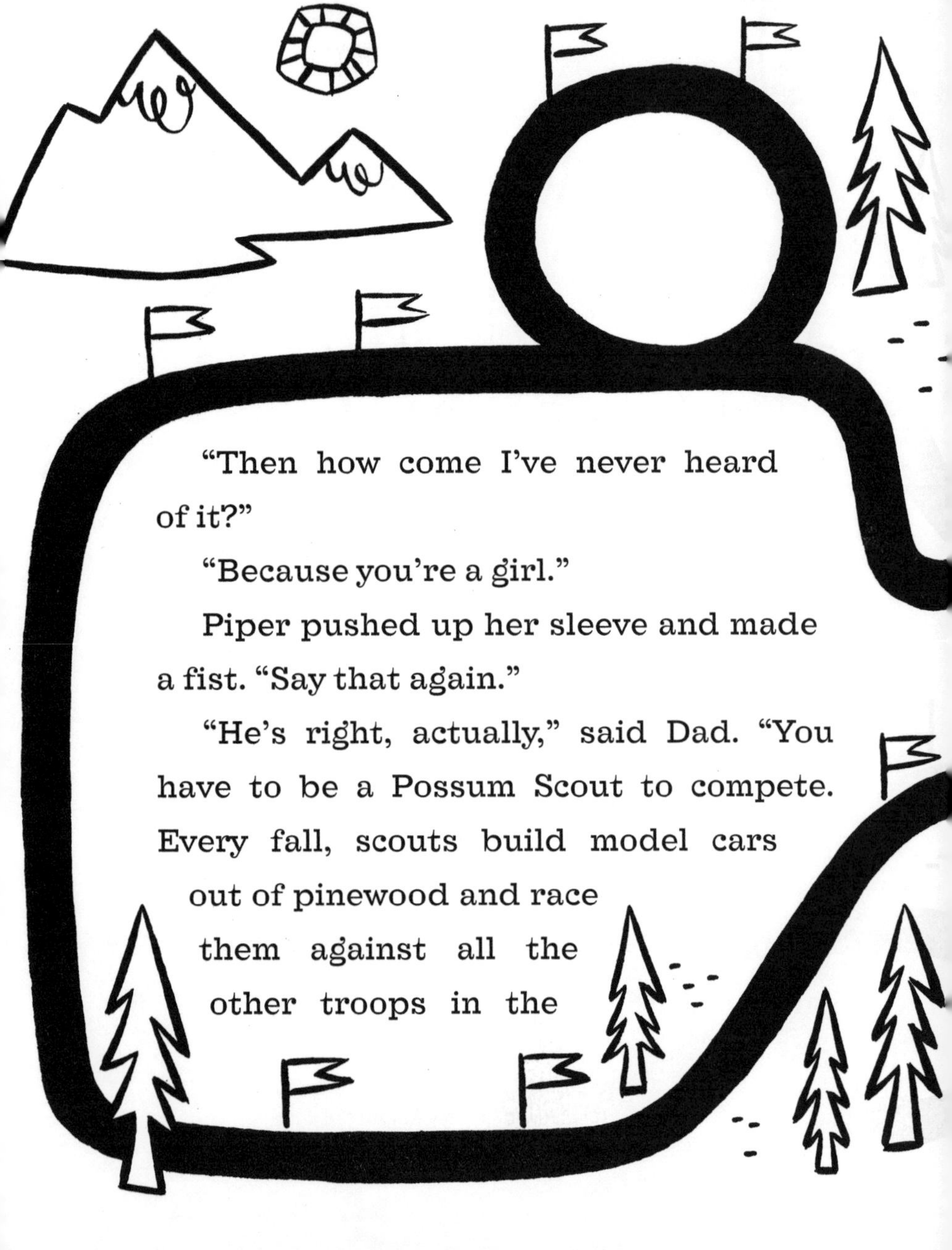

"Then how come I've never heard of it?"

"Because you're a girl."

Piper pushed up her sleeve and made a fist. "Say that again."

"He's right, actually," said Dad. "You have to be a Possum Scout to compete. Every fall, scouts build model cars out of pinewood and race them against all the other troops in the area. The '3000' stands for the three thousand inches of track used to make up the final race course."

"And the winner of the race is awarded five Possum Points," said Mom.

"Which is enough to advance me in rank from Pygmy to Shrew," said Frankie.

"But the race is this weekend," said Mom. "We're going to be out of town visiting your aunt Rachel."

Frankie and Dad looked at Mom with their best impression of sad puppies.

Mom sighed. "I'll call my sister and reschedule."

Dad looked at Frankie with a twinkle in his eye and

said, "I bet if we hurry, we can make it to the hobby shop and pick you up a car kit before it closes."

"You haven't even finished your dinner yet," said Mom.

"I'm full," said Frankie, giving Mom a drive-by hug as he rushed past her.

"Me too," said Dad as he kissed Mom on the cheek.

"But I made blueberry pie for dessert," said Mom.

Too late. Frankie and Dad were already pulling out of the driveway.

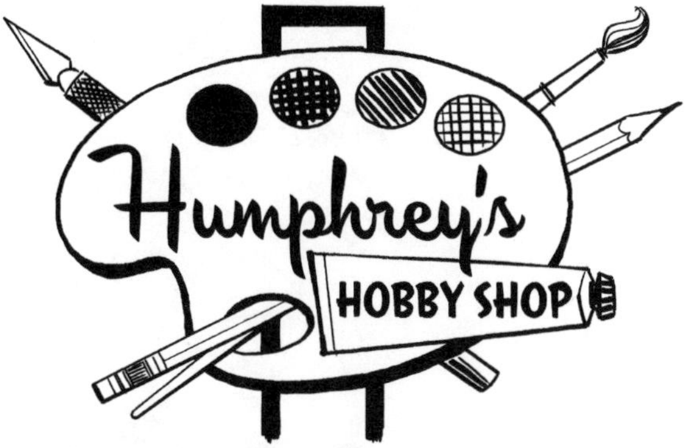
Humphrey's
HOBBY SHOP

CHAPTER FOUR

Humphrey's Hobby Shop was like a candy store for your brain. Whether you craved pom-poms or puffy paints, glue guns or glitter pens, every aisle was a rainbow assortment of do-it-yourself delights.

"There's no time to wander," said Dad. "The store closes in fifteen minutes."

"Sure thing," said Frankie. "I'm right behind yo—" Was that a rock polishing machine? Look at all those colors of felt. And pipe cleaners. And lawn gnomes. Who knew there were so many different kinds of googly eyes?

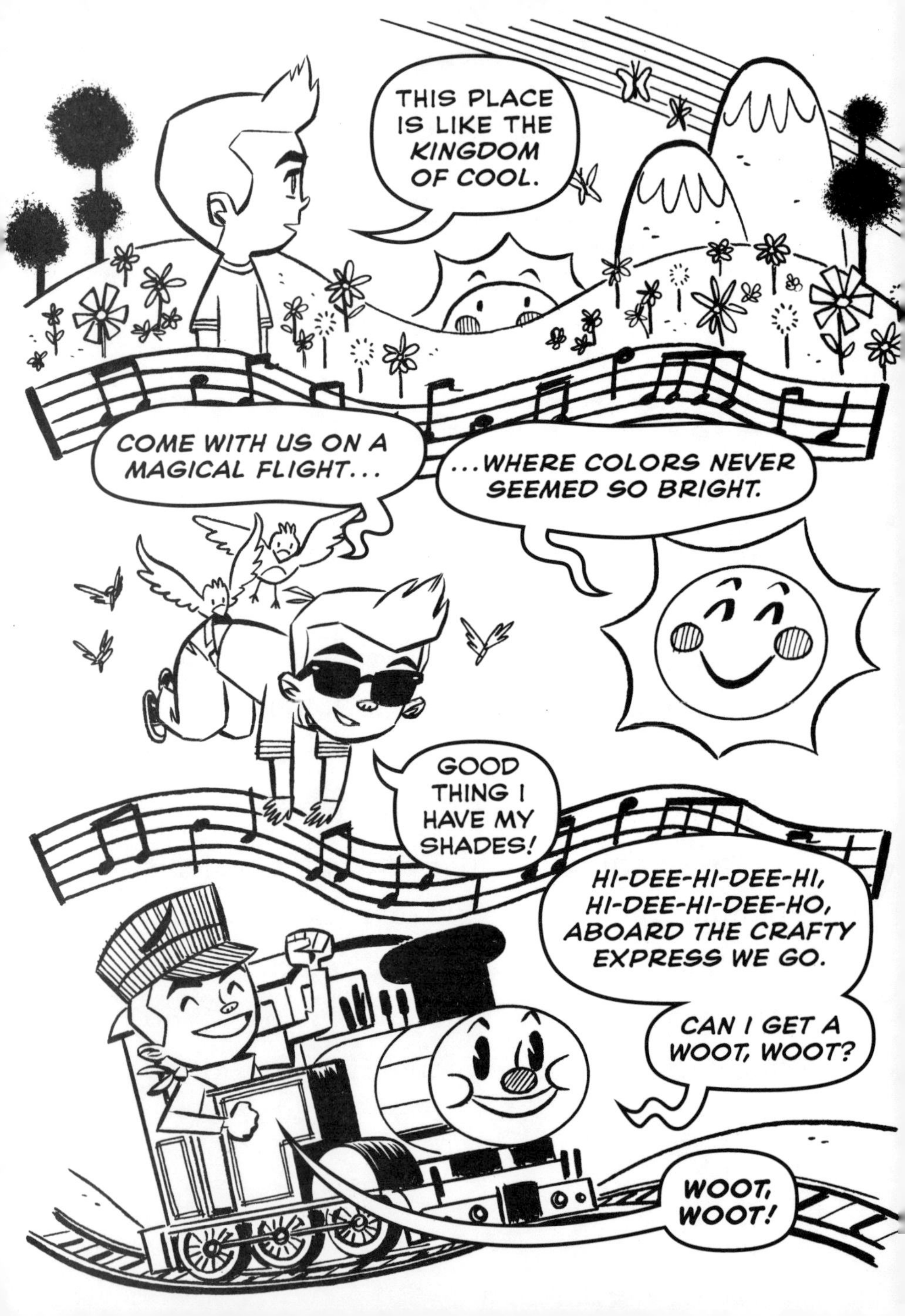
THIS PLACE IS LIKE THE *KINGDOM* OF COOL.
COME WITH US ON A MAGICAL FLIGHT...
...WHERE COLORS NEVER SEEMED SO BRIGHT.
GOOD THING I HAVE MY SHADES!
HI-DEE-HI-DEE-HI, HI-DEE-HI-DEE-HO, ABOARD THE CRAFTY EXPRESS WE GO.
CAN I GET A WOOT, WOOT?
WOOT, WOOT!

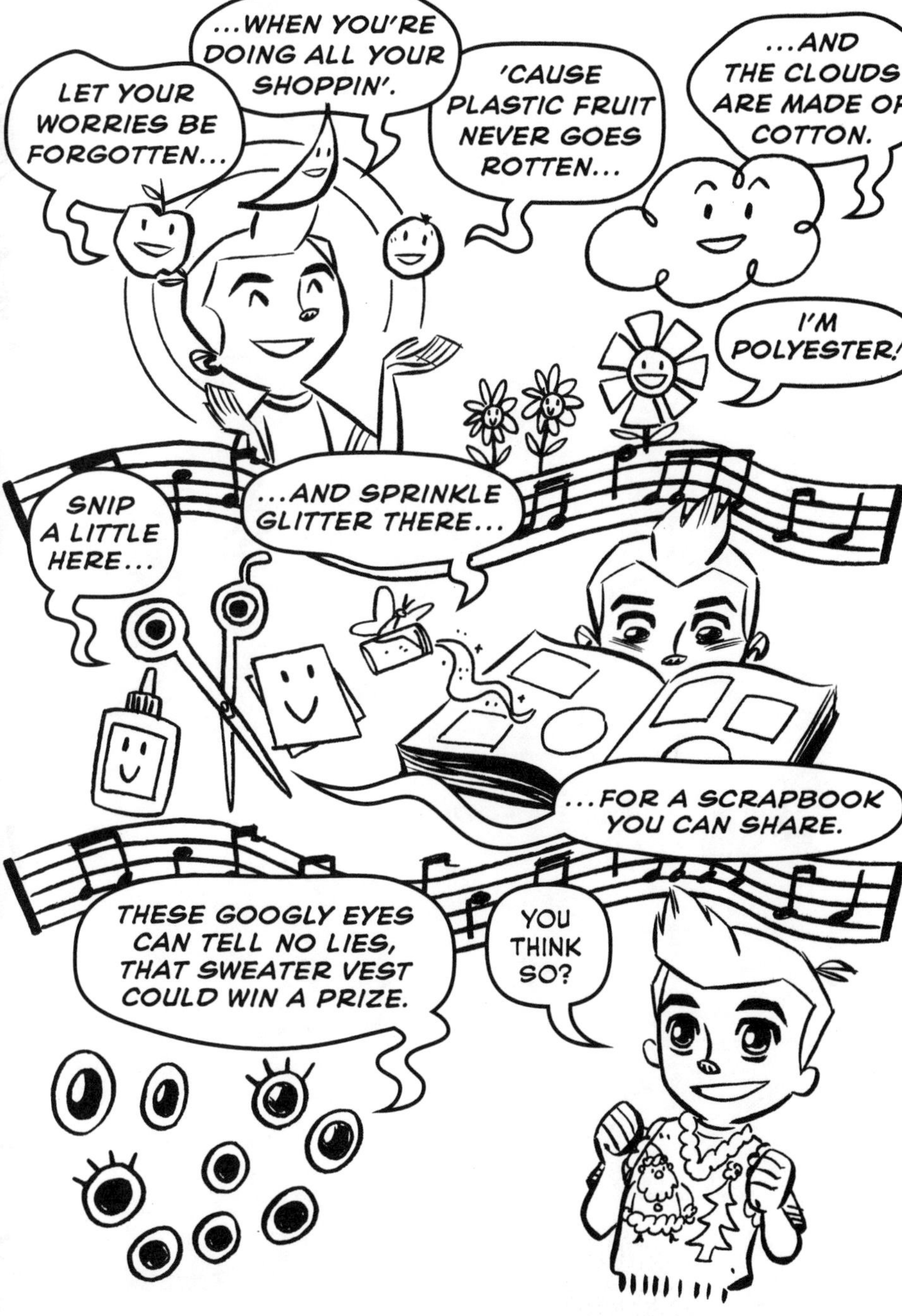
LET YOUR WORRIES BE FORGOTTEN...
...WHEN YOU'RE DOING ALL YOUR SHOPPIN'.
'CAUSE PLASTIC FRUIT NEVER GOES ROTTEN...
...AND THE CLOUDS ARE MADE OF COTTON.
I'M POLYESTER!
SNIP A LITTLE HERE...
...AND SPRINKLE GLITTER THERE...
...FOR A SCRAPBOOK YOU CAN SHARE.
THESE GOOGLY EYES CAN TELL NO LIES, THAT SWEATER VEST COULD WIN A PRIZE.
YOU THINK SO?

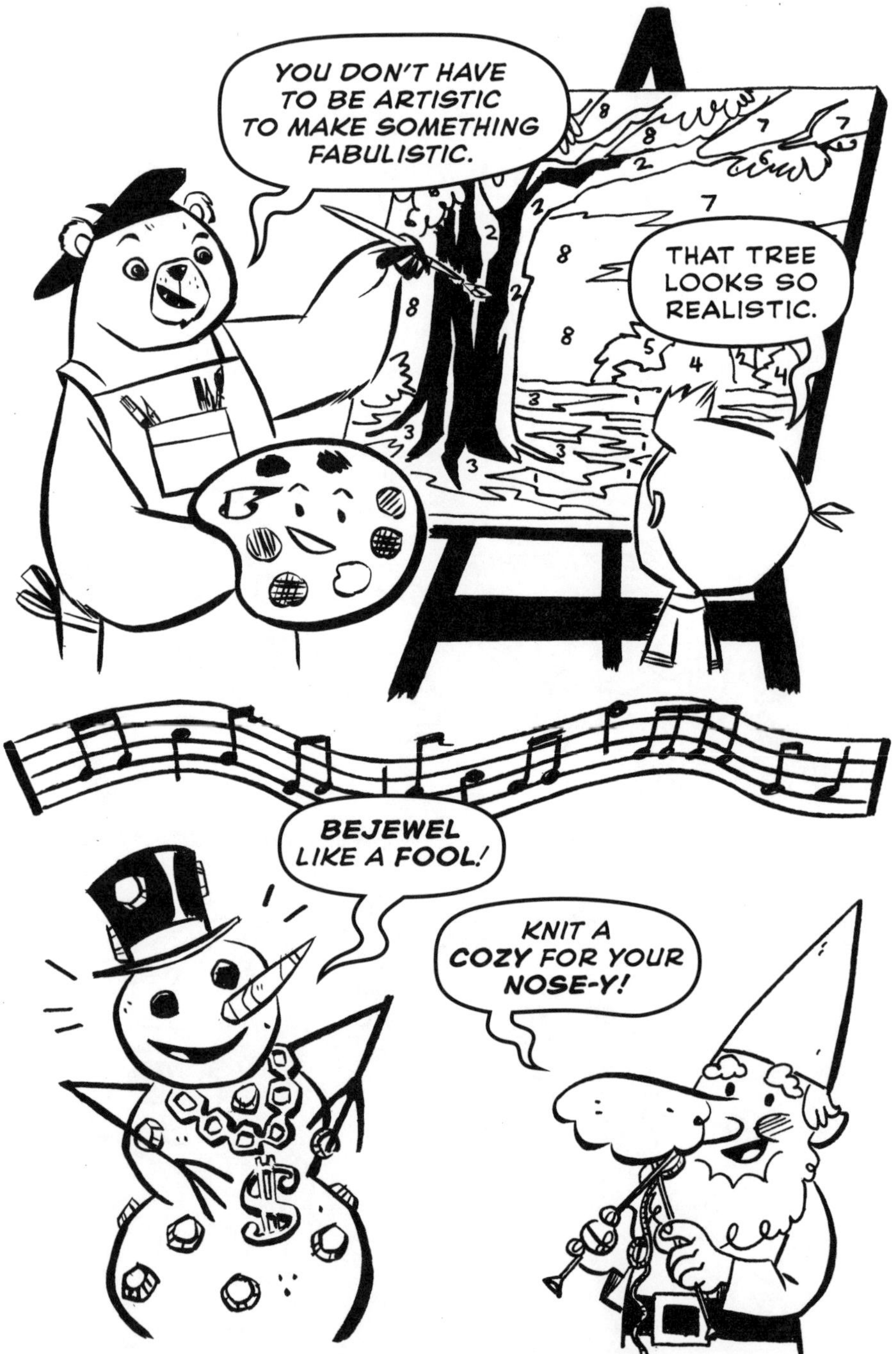
YOU DON'T HAVE TO BE ARTISTIC TO MAKE SOMETHING FABULISTIC.
THAT TREE LOOKS SO REALISTIC.
BEJEWEL LIKE A FOOL!
KNIT A COZY FOR YOUR NOSE-Y!

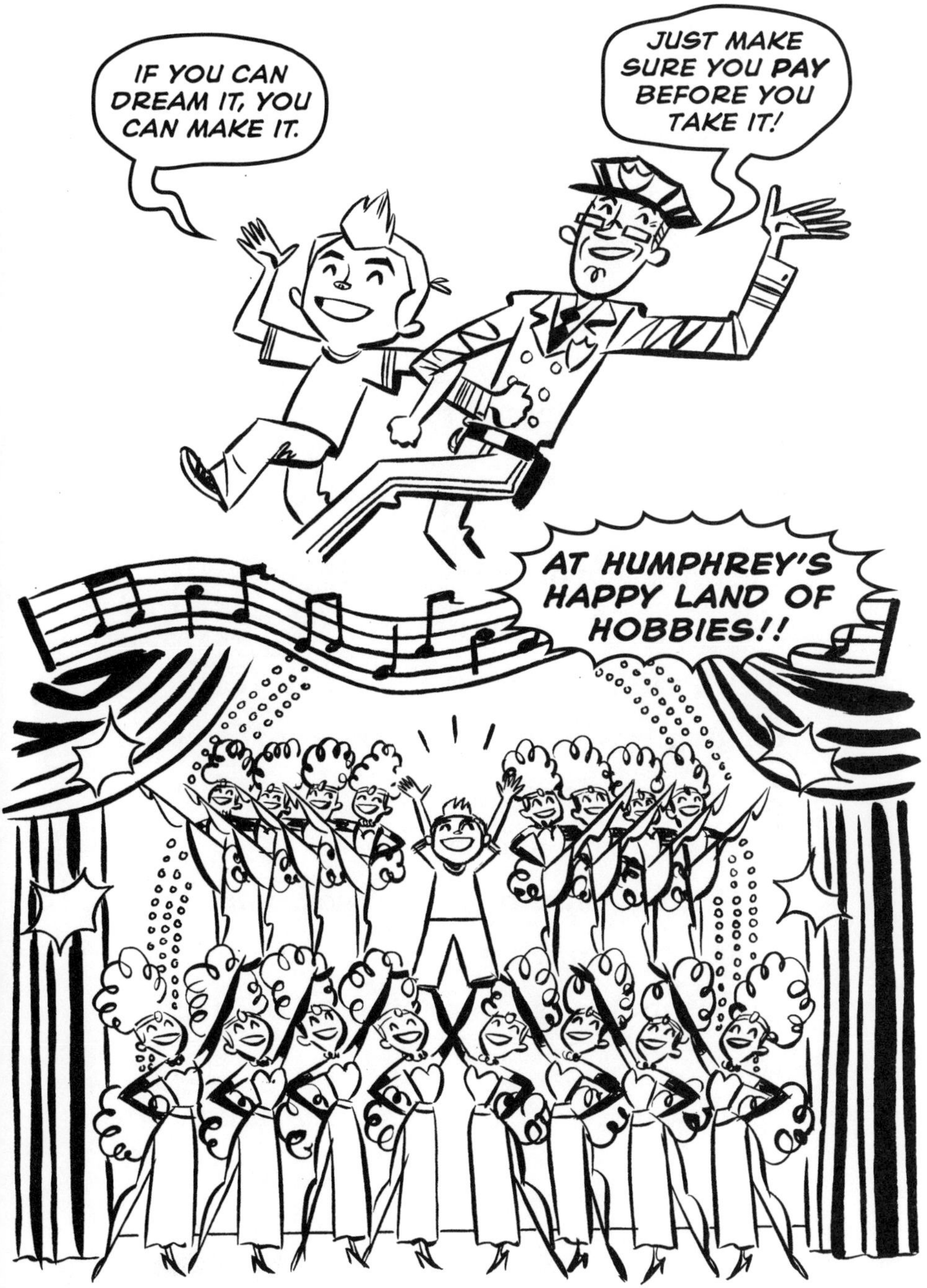
IF YOU CAN DREAM IT, YOU CAN MAKE IT.
JUST MAKE SURE YOU PAY BEFORE YOU TAKE IT!
AT HUMPHREY'S HAPPY LAND OF HOBBIES!!

"Are you dancing with that statue?" said Dad.

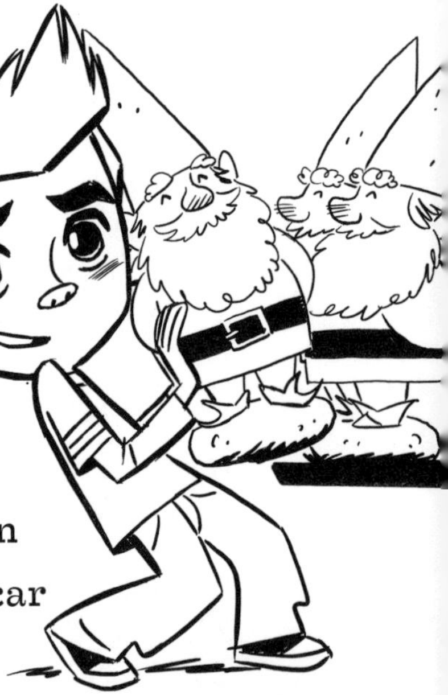

"Um, no?" said Frankie, casually returning the lawn gnome to the shelf.

Dad steered Frankie in the direction of the race-car kits. Humphrey's didn't disappoint. There were dozens of models on display. Some looked like sport coupes, others were shaped like dragsters. Some barely looked like cars at all.

"Things sure have changed since I was your age," said Dad. "There are so many different kinds. It's going to be hard to decide."

"I want this one," said Frankie. He

pulled a car with a sleek, curvy design off the shelf.

"That's pretty slick," said Dad. "But it looks kind of flimsy. How about something with a little more—"

"Nope, this is the one," said Frankie, holding firmly to the speedster.

"Don't you want my help picking it out?"

"I already found it."

With only two minutes until closing, Dad reluctantly bought the race-car kit. Frankie was on his way to the starting line.

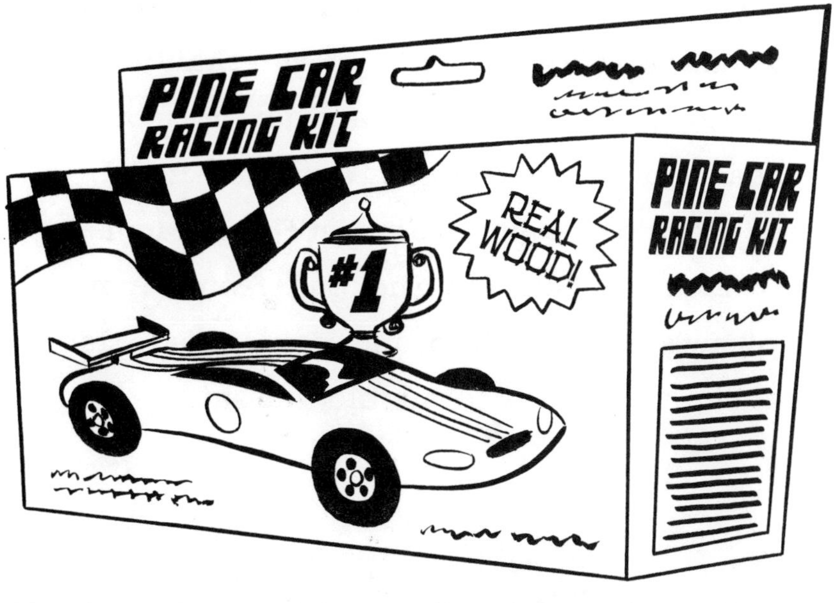
PINE CAR
RACING KIT
REAL
WOOD!
#1
PINE CAR
RACING KIT

CHAPTER FIVE

By the time Frankie and Dad returned home, the girls were all settled in for the night. Lucy was drifting asleep as she snuggled her favorite stuffed monkey. Piper was in bed, reading a book about a girl with a crush on a vampire basketball player. And Mom was relaxing in her favorite chair with a mug of chamomile tea and an old movie that had plenty of singing and smooching.

"How'd you guys make out?" said Mom.

Frankie held up the bag from Humphrey's Hobby Shop and gave it a little shake. "I'm ready to rumble," he said.

"No rumbling until the morning," said Mom. "It's time for bed."

"We'll work on it together first thing tomorrow," said Dad.

"But I want to build it on my own," said Frankie.

"Oh." Dad deflated like a balloon. "Well, maybe you'll change your mind when you wake up."

Frankie hugged and kissed his parents good night, then went up to his room. On the way to his bed he almost tripped over a white ball of fur. Argyle uncurled himself, rolling onto his back to have his belly rubbed.

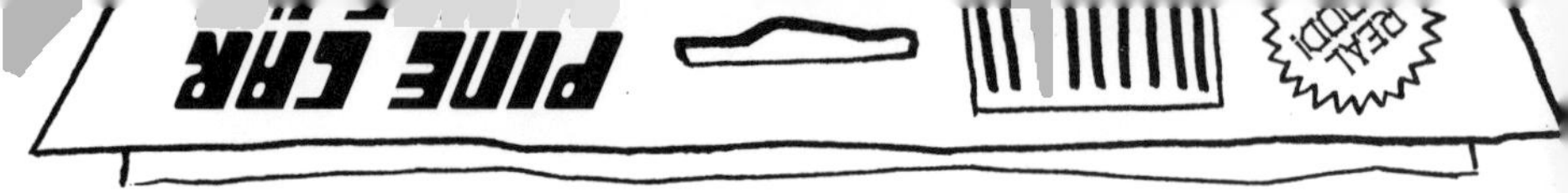

"No time for that, Pooch. I have to rest up for an important mission," said Frankie.

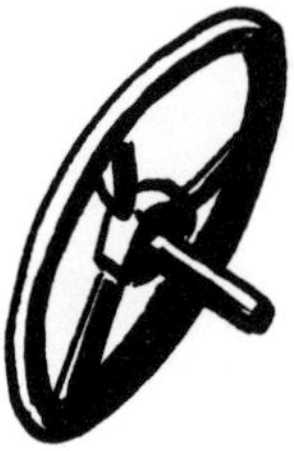

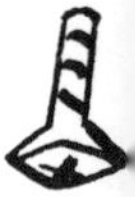

He threw on his pajamas and hopped under the covers with the bag from Humphrey's. Tired as he was, there was no way Frankie could wait until morning to see what was inside the race-car kit. He tore open the box. And ripped the directions in half. Oops.

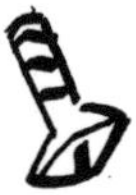

Won't need those, anyway, he thought. He spilled the pieces onto his comforter. There was a wedge of wood, wheels, axles, turbo vents, paints, decals, and even a miniature driver. Everything to build the winning race car.

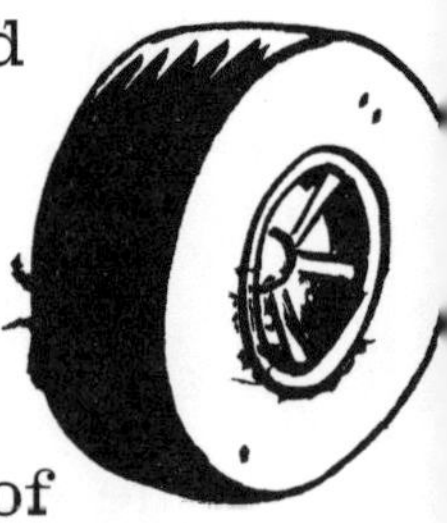

"Awwwesome," said Frankie with a yawn. Then he drifted asleep under a blanket of car parts.

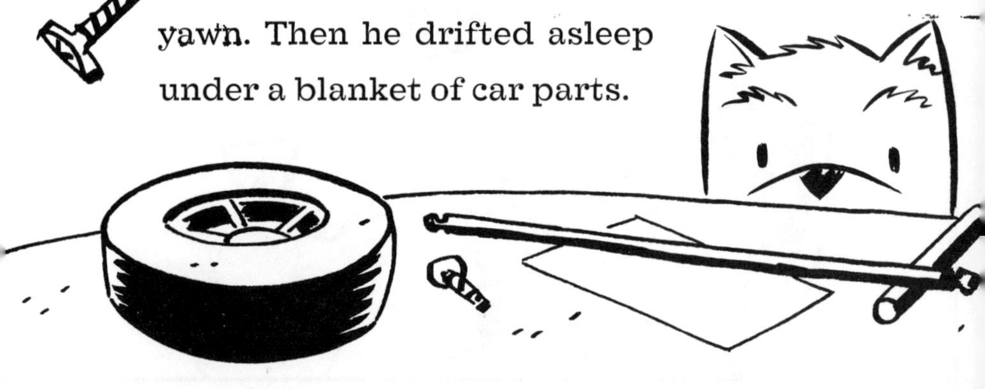

CHAPTER SIX

There was a knock on Frankie's door.

"Morning, Champ," said Dad. "Just checking to see if you wanted any help."

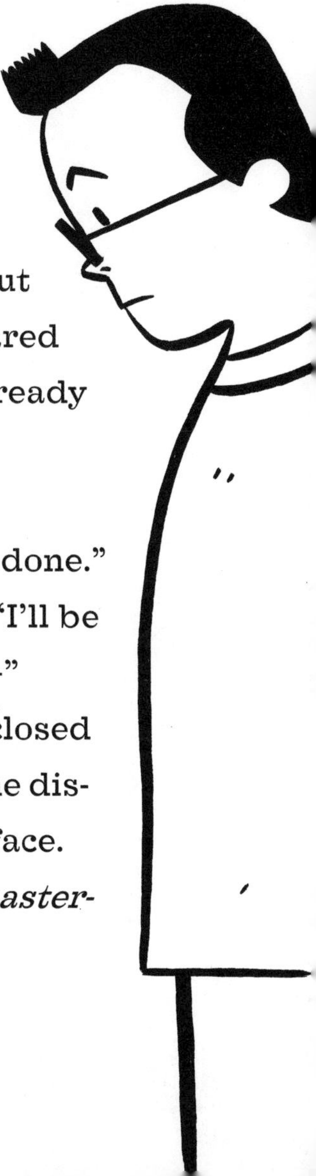

Frankie poked his head out of his room. His face was smeared with grease. "No thanks. I'm already off to a great start."

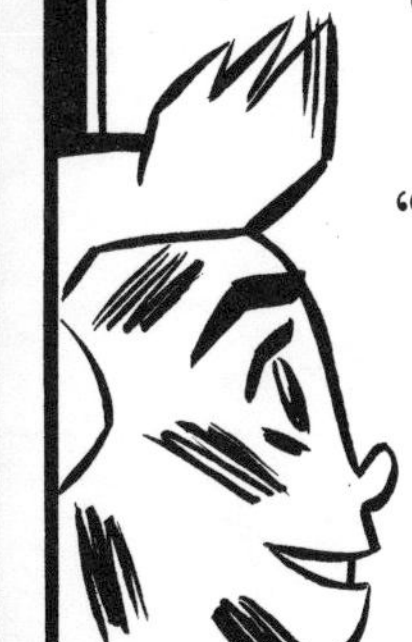

"Can I at least see it?"

"Sorry, no peeking till it's done."

"All right," said Dad. "I'll be downstairs if you nee—"

"I won't." Frankie closed his door, not noticing the disappointed look on Dad's face.

And now to complete my masterpiece, Frankie thought.

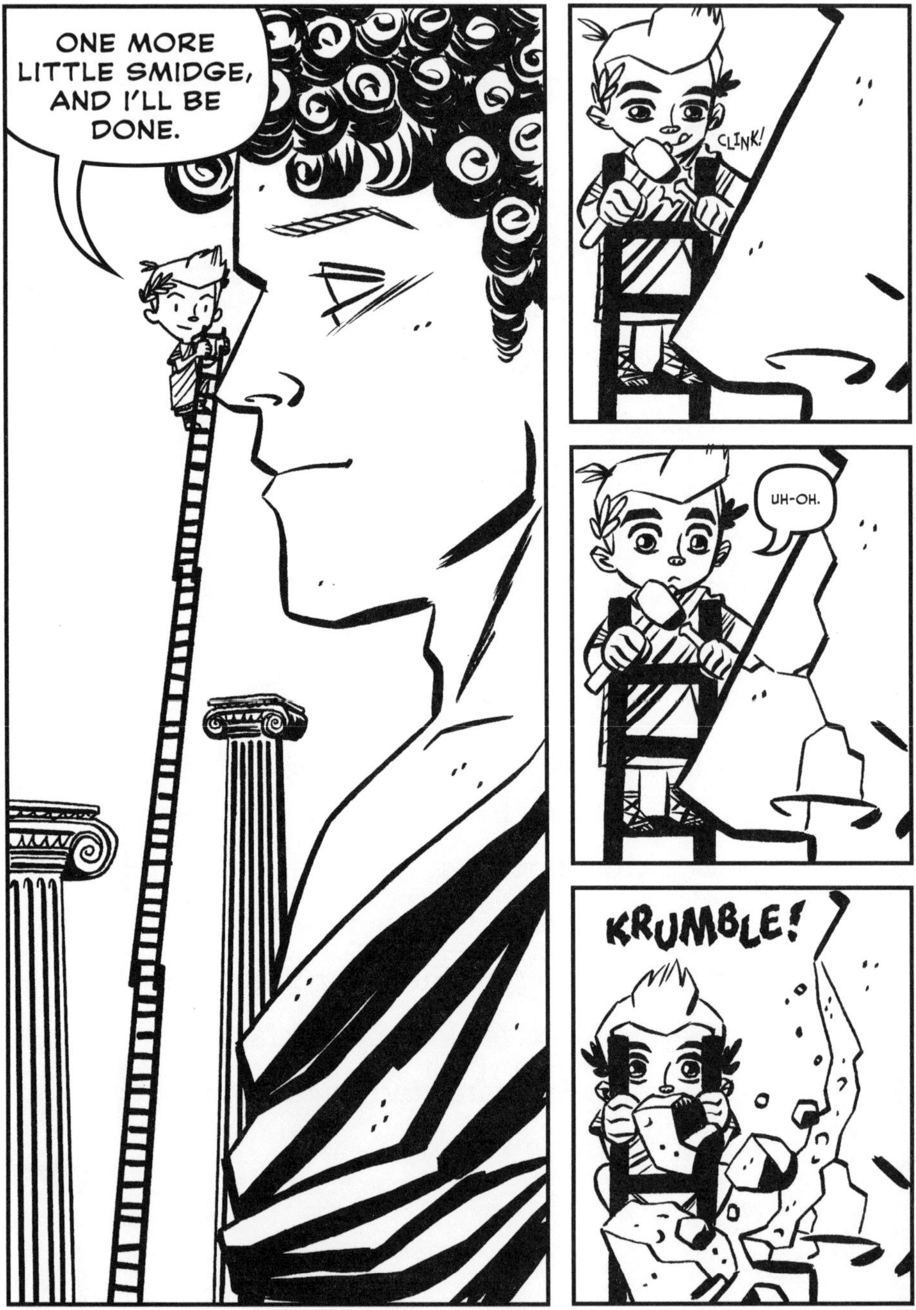
ONE MORE LITTLE SMIDGE, AND I'LL BE DONE.
CLINK!
UH-OH.
KRUMBLE!

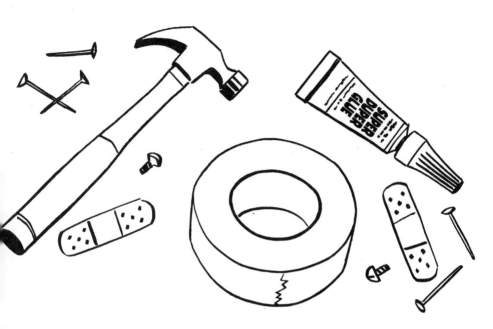

CHAPTER SEVEN

Frankie had somehow managed to snap off the nose of his car. Oh well, nothing a little glue couldn't fix. And some duct tape. And maybe some Spackle.

He went downstairs to get the supplies to repair his car.

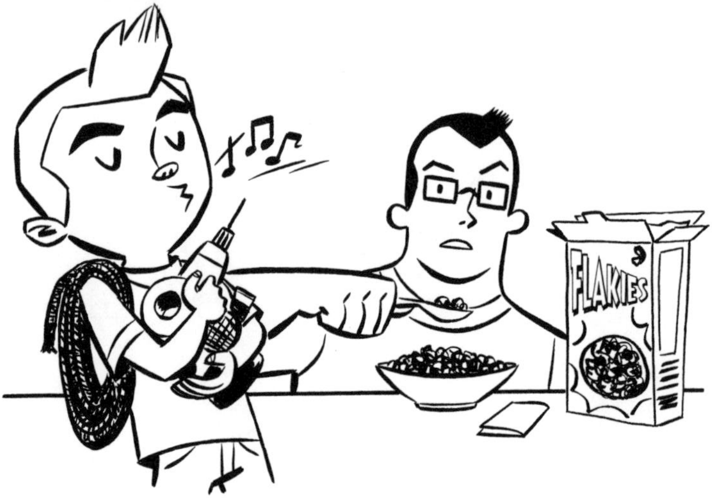
FLAKIES

Dad looked up from his bowl of corn-flakes. "How's it coming along?" he said. "Ready to take that car out for a spin?"

"Just about," said Frankie. "Do we have any Spackle?"

"Next to the paint rollers. Anything I can help you with?"

"I'm good," said Frankie. "Nothing worth getting your cereal soggy over."

"Okeydokey." Dad sighed.

Frankie gathered everything he needed and returned to his room. He went to work gluing and duct taping and spackling his race car. Before long it was finished. Maybe he should have waited for the Spackle to set before he painted it, but he was sure the colors would be less streaky once the car had dried.

Frankie took a step back to admire his handiwork.

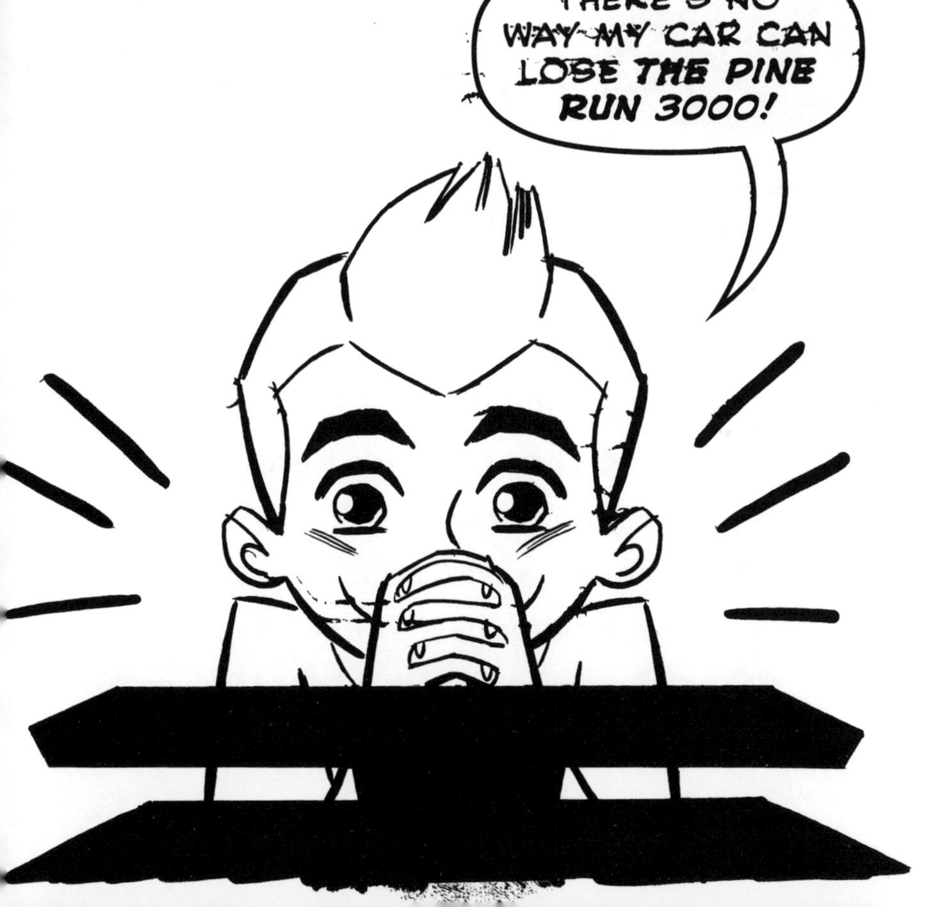
THERE'S NO WAY MY CAR CAN LOSE THE PINE RUN 3000!

CHAPTER EIGHT

Frankie couldn't wait to show off his masterpiece to the other Possum Scouts. But when he got on the school bus the next morning, the other kids were already crowded around Carter.

"It's so shiny," said Kevin.

"Look at that spoiler," said Oliver.

"Those flames are wicked," said Lucas.

"Flames are so predictable," said Frankie. Did he say that out loud?

"What's your problem, Pickle?" said Carter.

"I don't have a problem," said Frankie. "I'm the one who's going to win the Pine Run 3000."

The other kids all gasped. Oliver choked on his spit.

"How do you know that?" said Carter.

"Because I'm racing THIS!"

The boys all started to laugh at Frankie's car. Not the reaction Frankie was hoping for.

"That paint job is all gloopy," said Kevin.

"It looks like someone stepped on it," said Oliver.

"Are those rainbows on the side?" said Lucas.

"Those are laser beams," said Frankie. "And I still say my car is faster than Carter's."

"Maybe we should race them today and find out," said Carter.

"How about recess?" said Frankie. "Winner gets pudding."

"You're on," said Carter.

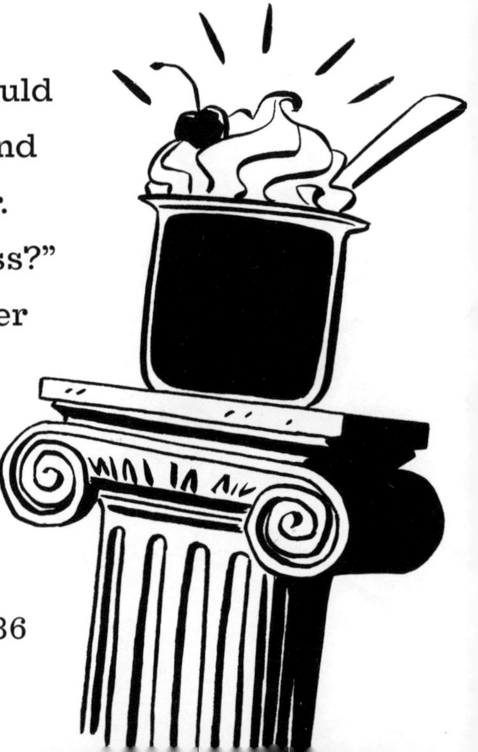

CHAPTER NINE

Challenging Carter to a race seemed like a great idea in the moment. But as the morning crept on, Frankie wasn't so sure. Carter's car did look *really* awesome.

Recess arrived. The kids all crowded around the jungle gym to make sure they had a good view. Word had traveled so fast that even the other grades were there to watch.

Frankie looked over at Kenny and said, "You think I have a shot at winning this, right?"

Kenny whistled a sound like a bomb being dropped.

Not good.

Frankie and Carter agreed that the corkscrew slide was the best spot to race. They climbed up the ladder together and lined up their cars on the slide's edge.

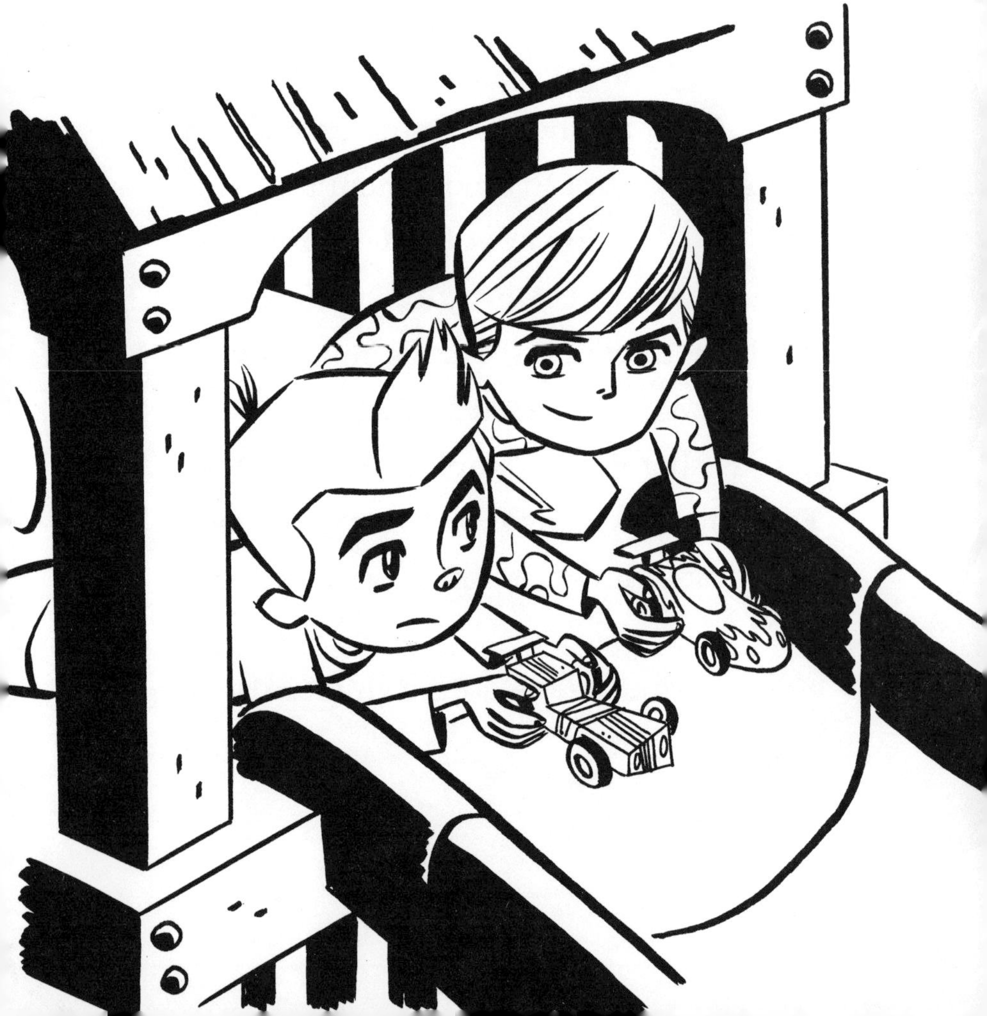

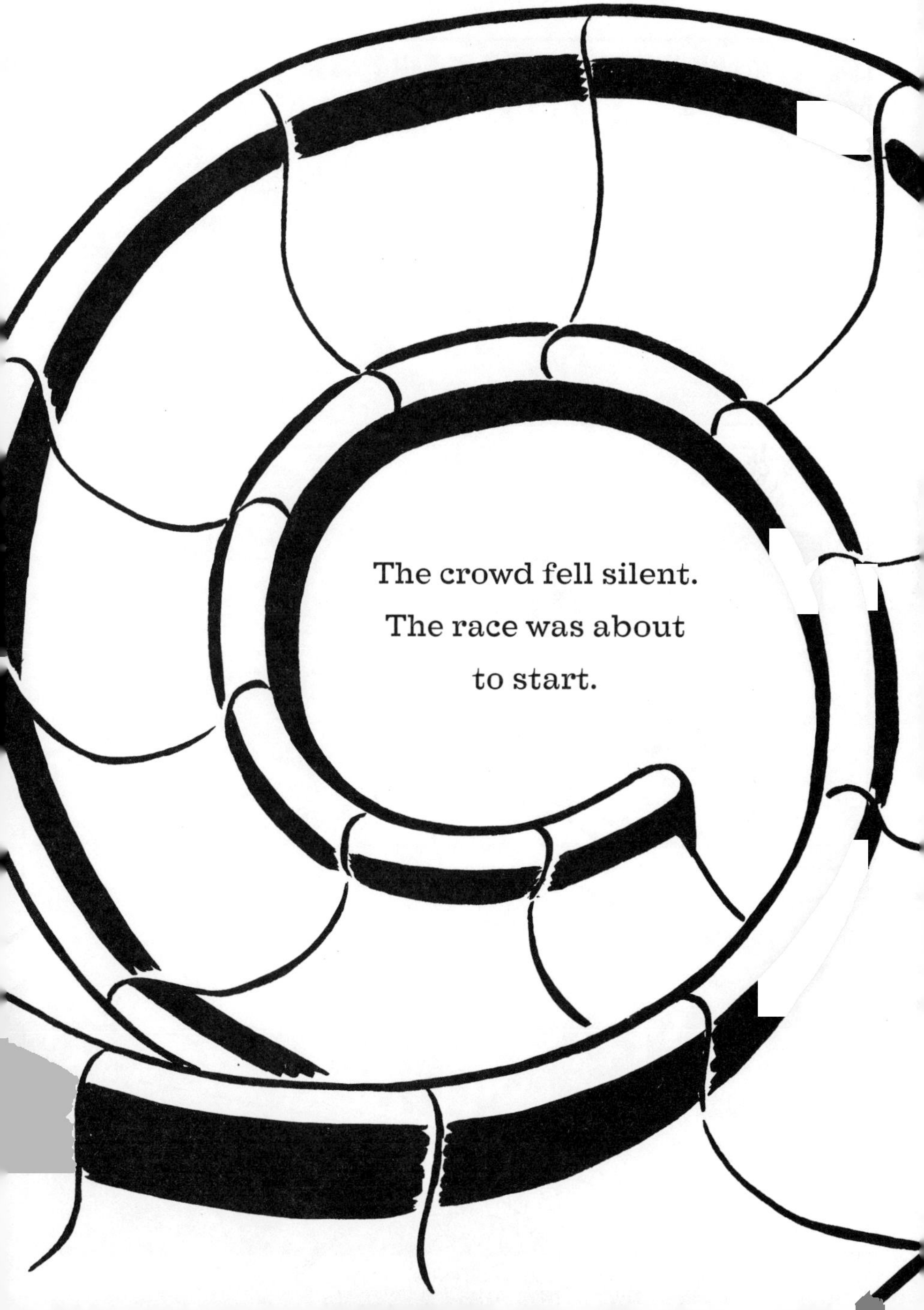

The crowd fell silent.
The race was about
to start.

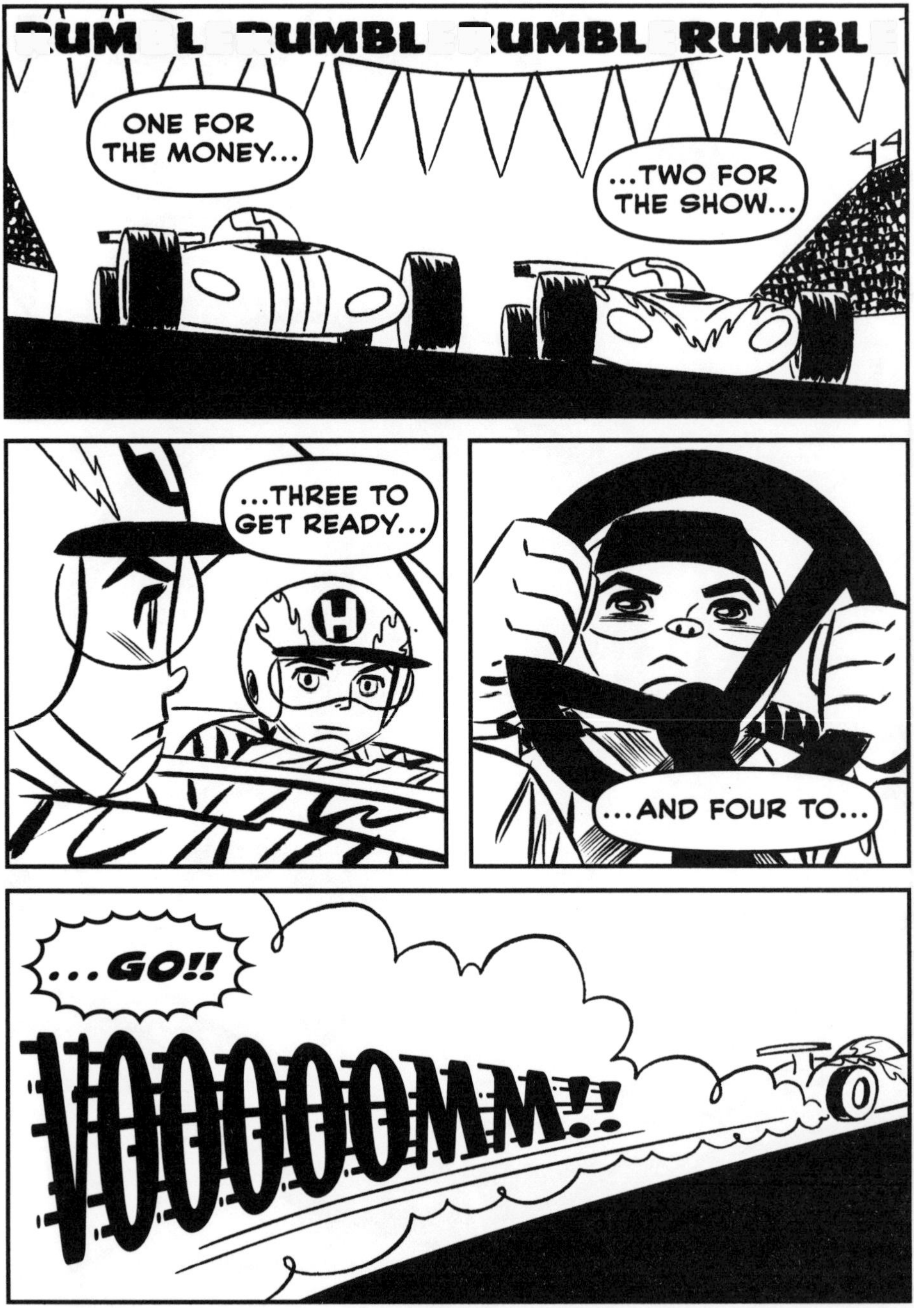
UM L UMBL UMBL RUMBL
ONE FOR THE MONEY...
...TWO FOR THE SHOW...
...THREE TO GET READY...
...AND FOUR TO...
...GO!!
VOOOOOMM!!

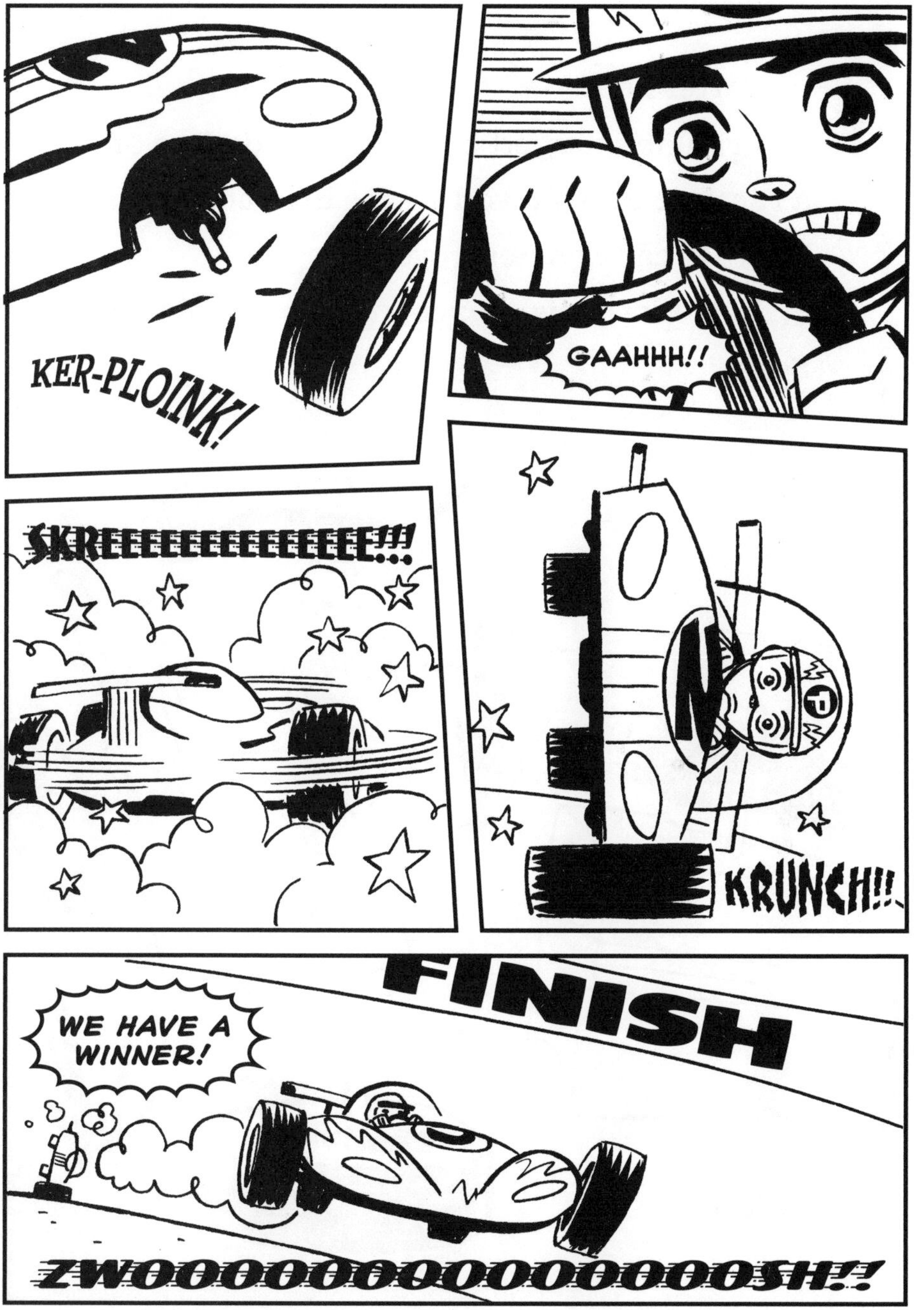
KER-PLOINK!
GAAHHH!!
SKREEEEEEEEEEEEEEE!!!
KRUNCH!!!
FINISH
WE HAVE A WINNER!
ZWOOOOOOOOOOOOOOOOSH!!

Carter had won.

Frankie scooped up his jumbled mess of a race car and shoved it into his backpack. His race car was destroyed.

He'd blown his chance to become a Shrew Scout.

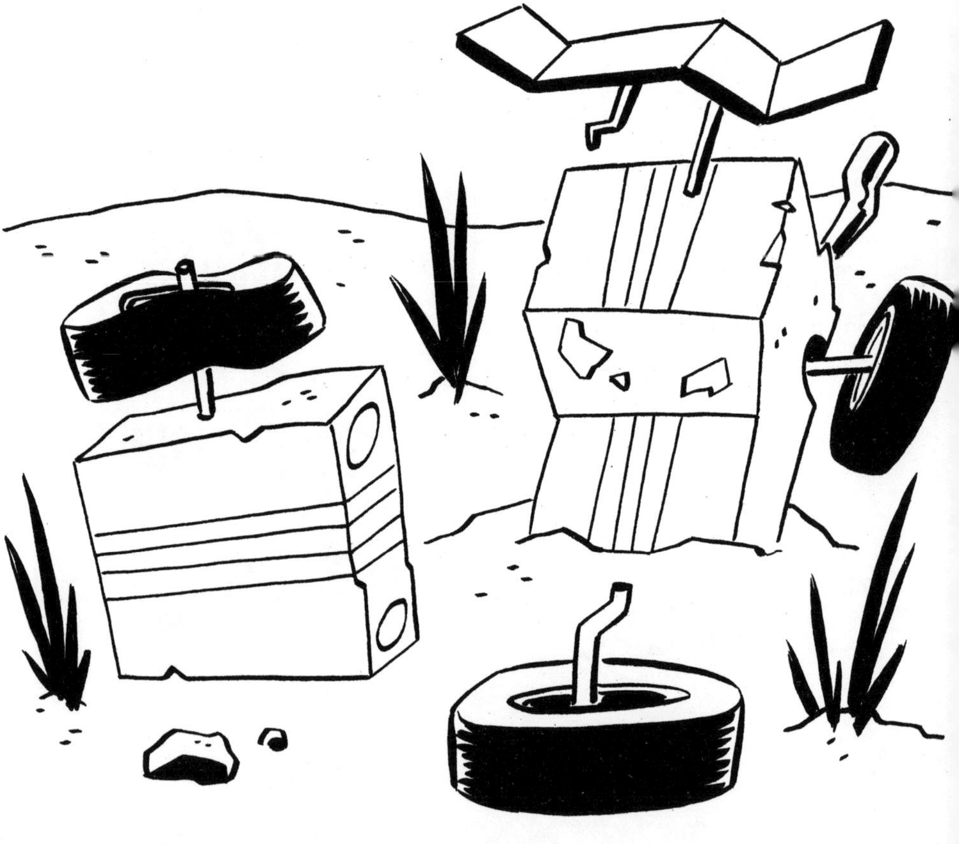

CHAPTER TEN

Frankie was in a total funk. Nothing could cheer him up. Not even being home from school, or Dad's secret stash of oatmeal-and-chocolate-covered raisin cookies, or a marathon of his favorite TV show, *Mega Morphin' Mutant Monsters*. There was no way he'd be able to race in the Pine Run 3000.

Maybe he could design a new car. He got out his sketch pad and some markers, and went to work drawing the coolest race car

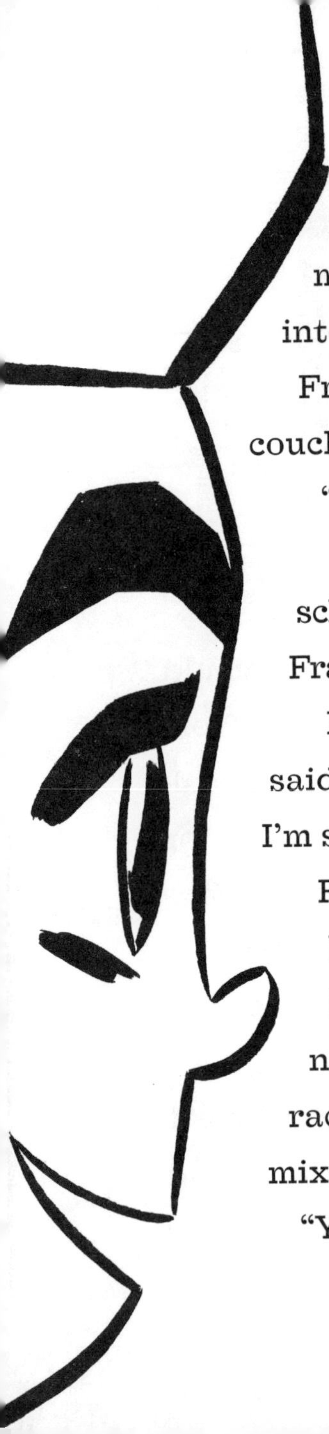

he could imagine. If only he could wave the marker like a magic wand and turn his picture into a reality.

Frankie was a droopy lump on the couch when Dad got home.

"Why so glum, Chum?" said Dad.

"I kind of crashed my car at school." As the words came out, Frankie started to cry.

Dad put his arm around him and said, "Why don't we have a look at it. I'm sure it's not as bad as you think."

Frankie spilled the contents of his backpack onto the kitchen table.

It wasn't pretty. There were definitely still parts that looked like a race car, but everything was sort of mixed-up and smooshed together.

"Yowzers," said Dad.

"See, I told you," said Frankie as he wiped his nose on his sleeve.

"Follow me," said Dad. "I want to show you something."

Dad led Frankie downstairs into the basement. Past the boxes of Christmas decorations and unwanted heirlooms was a door. Frankie knew it well. It was the one part of the house only Dad was allowed to enter. Not even Mom had access.

And now Frankie was about to go inside.

X-MAS

FRAGILE

KEEP
OUT!

CHAPTER ELEVEN

If dad was king, this room was definitely his castle.

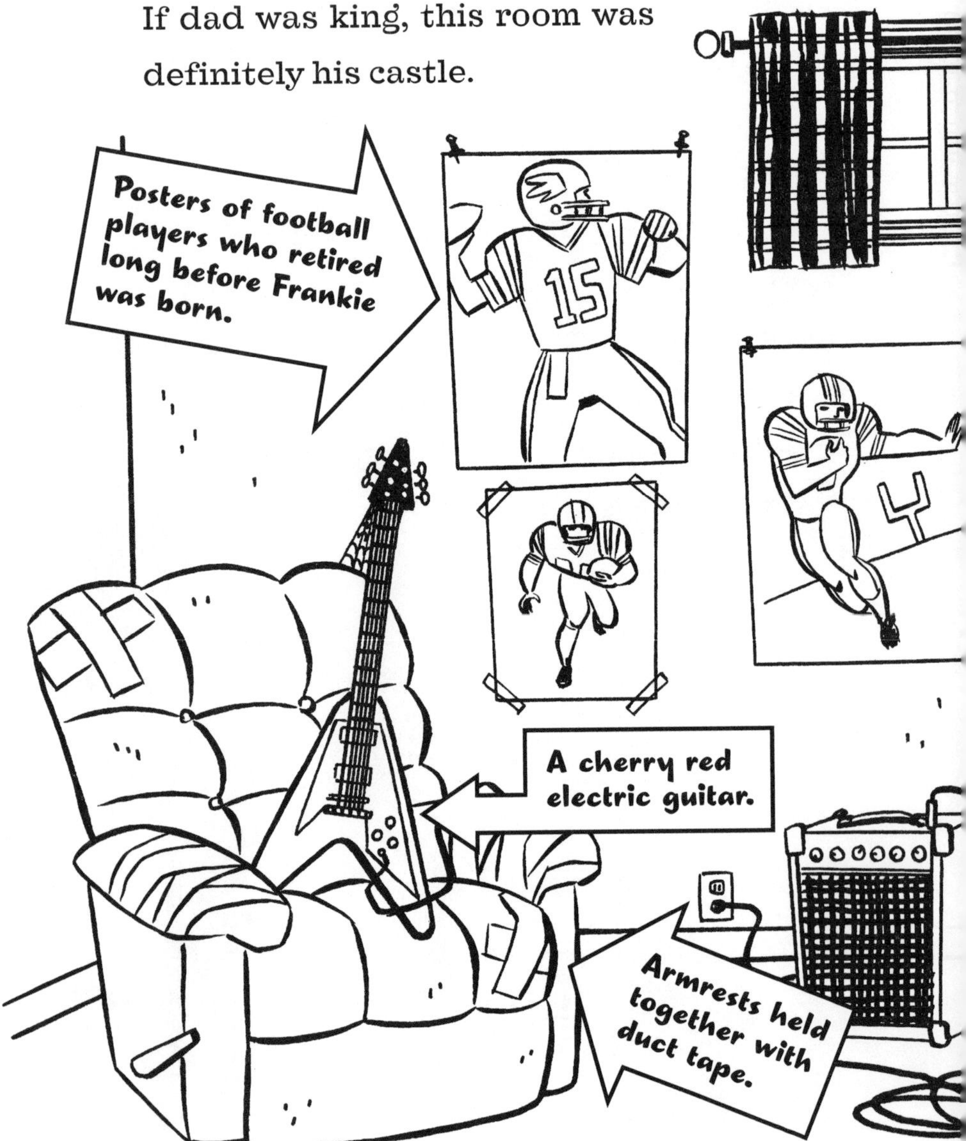
Posters of football players who retired long before Frankie was born.
15
A cherry red electric guitar.
Armrests held together with duct tape.

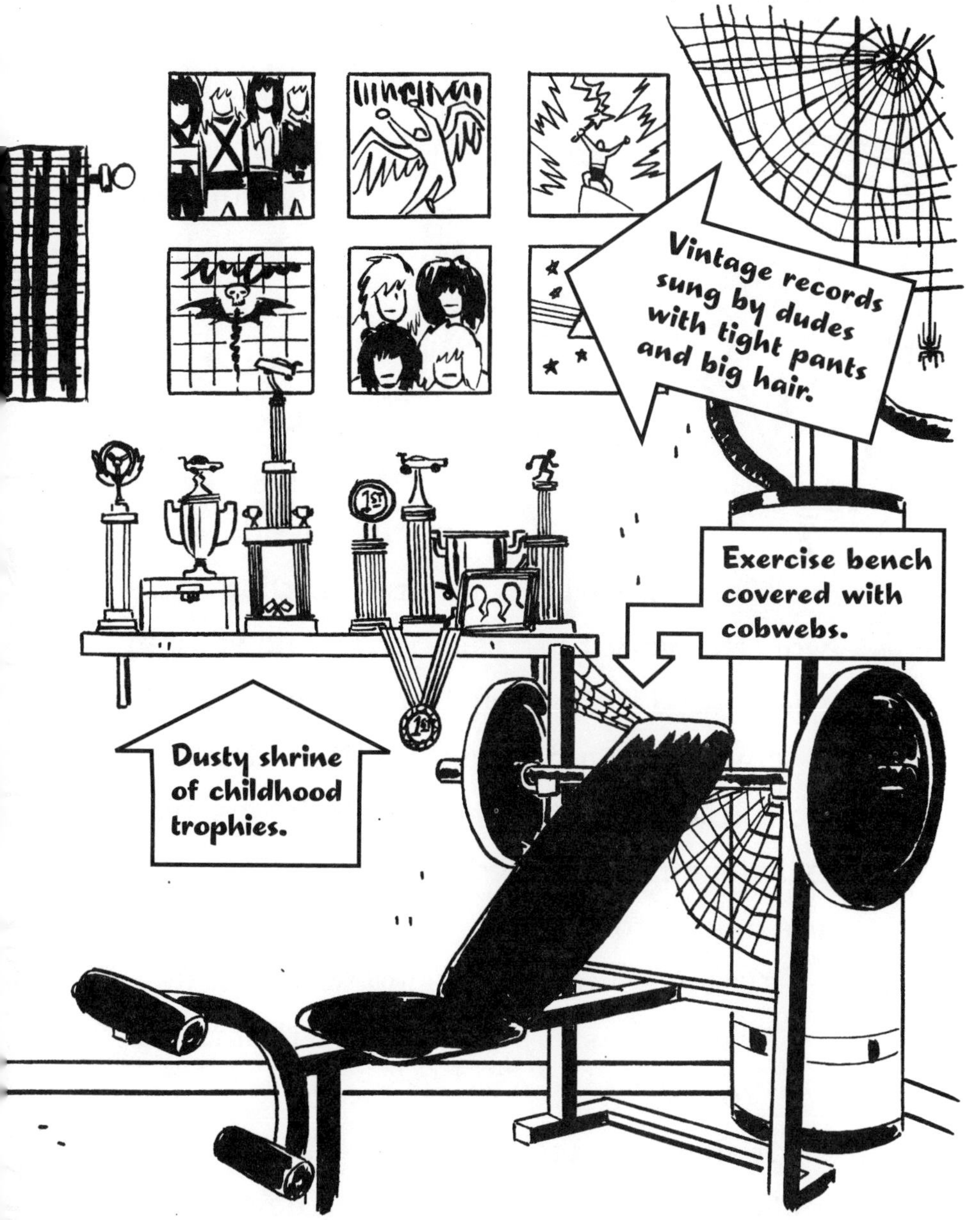
Vintage records sung by dudes with tight pants and big hair.
Exercise bench covered with cobwebs.
Dusty shrine of childhood trophies.

Frankie suddenly realized why no one else was allowed in this room. This was Dad's very own Hall of Awesome.

Dad took one of the trophies from the shelf and blew off the dust. It looked heavy enough to be made of lead.

"This one was your grandfather's. He won the very first race in '53. Back then they called it the 'Pine Run Steeplechase.'"

"Sweet," said Frankie. Dad let him hold the trophy for a little bit. It was even heavier than it looked. "Who do all the others belong to?"

"They're mine," Dad said with a smile.

Frankie wasn't sure he heard that right. "Yours?"

It all started to make sense. The engravings on the trophies. The newspaper clippings. The photographs of his dad and grandpa in their scout uniforms, shaking hands with important-looking people.

Frankie's family was two generations of Pine Run champions.

Dad placed the trophy back on the shelf and traded it for a wooden box that looked like the kind of thing you kept cigars in. Inside was a car that resembled an old-fashioned hot rod.

"Is that what you won all these trophies with?" said Frankie.

"Your grandfather helped me build it, just like his dad helped him build his race car."

"Why didn't you tell me?"

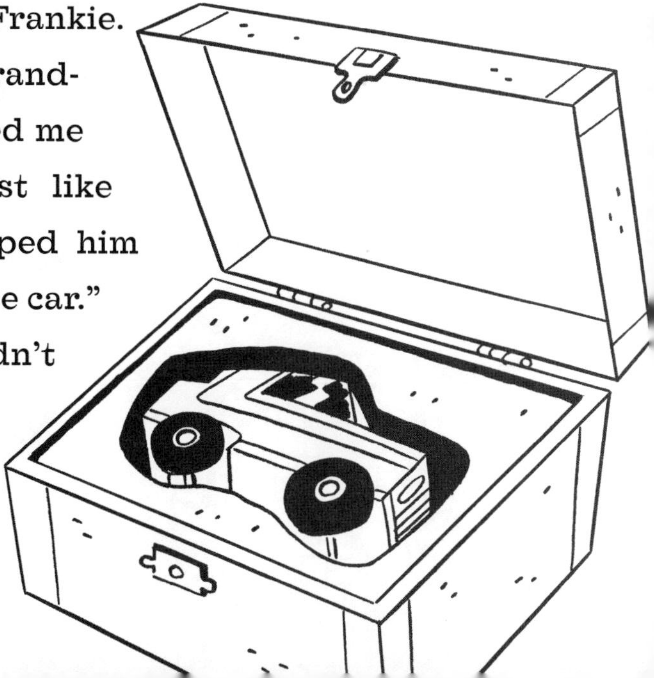

"You wanted to do this on your own."

"Yeah, that didn't go quite like I had planned," said Frankie. "Can you help me become a champion, like you and Grandpa?"

Dad had that twinkle in his eye again.

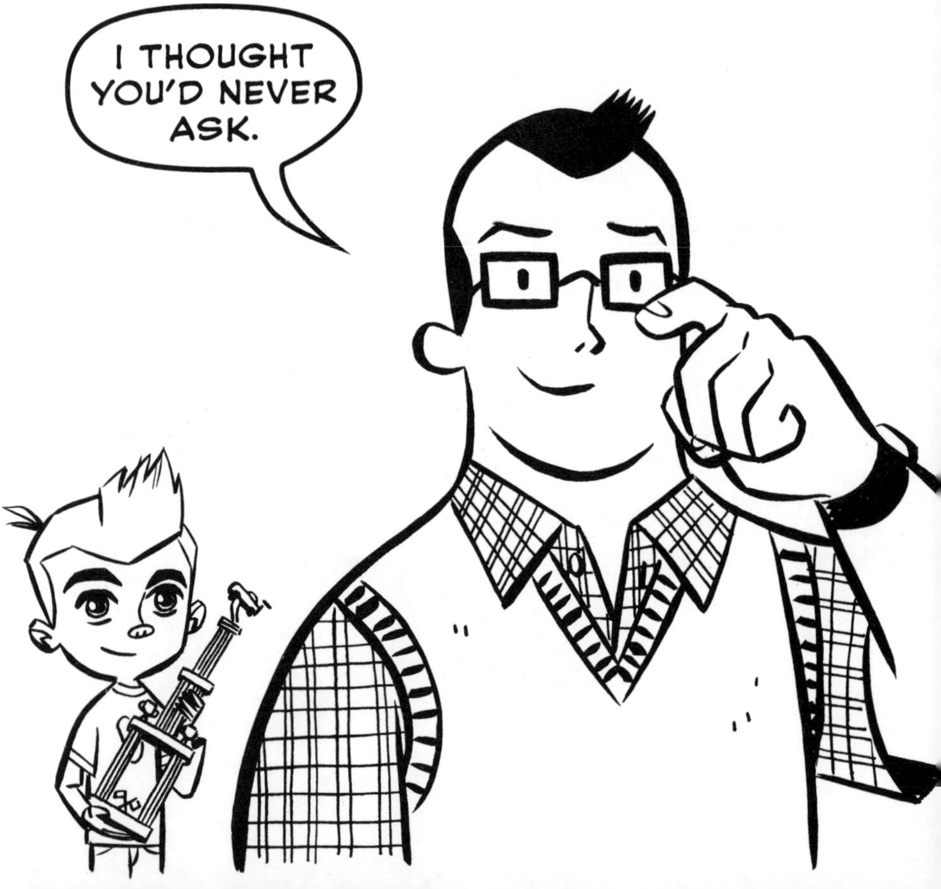
I THOUGHT YOU'D NEVER ASK.

CHAPTER TWELVE

With Dad helping him, there was no way Frankie could lose the Pine Run 3000. There was only one teensy-weensy problem: his car. Or what was left of it.

"Don't worry," said Dad. "We can rebuild it together. Make it better. Faster."

Frankie grabbed his sketch pad and showed Dad his new race-car design. "How about spiffier?"

Dad examined Frankie's drawing.

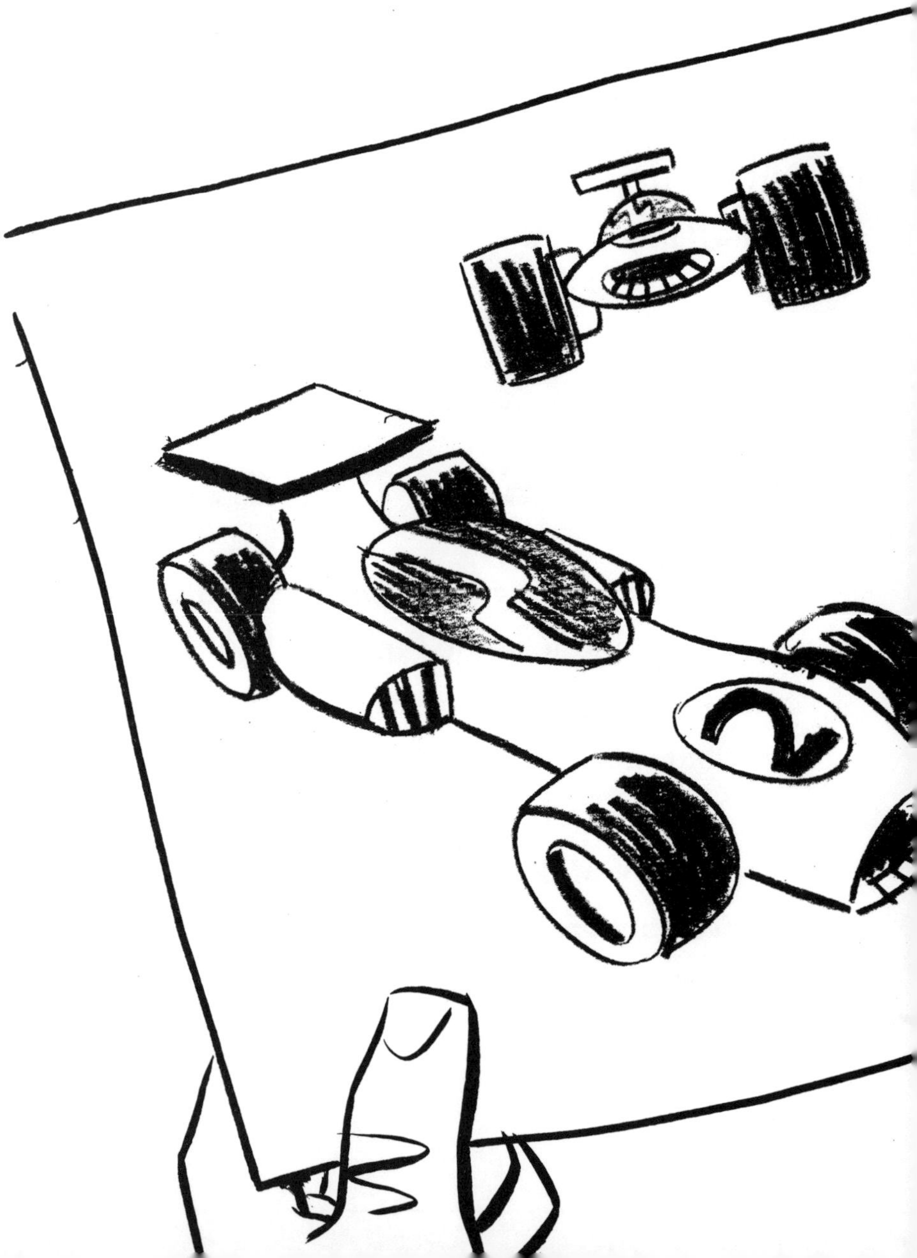

2

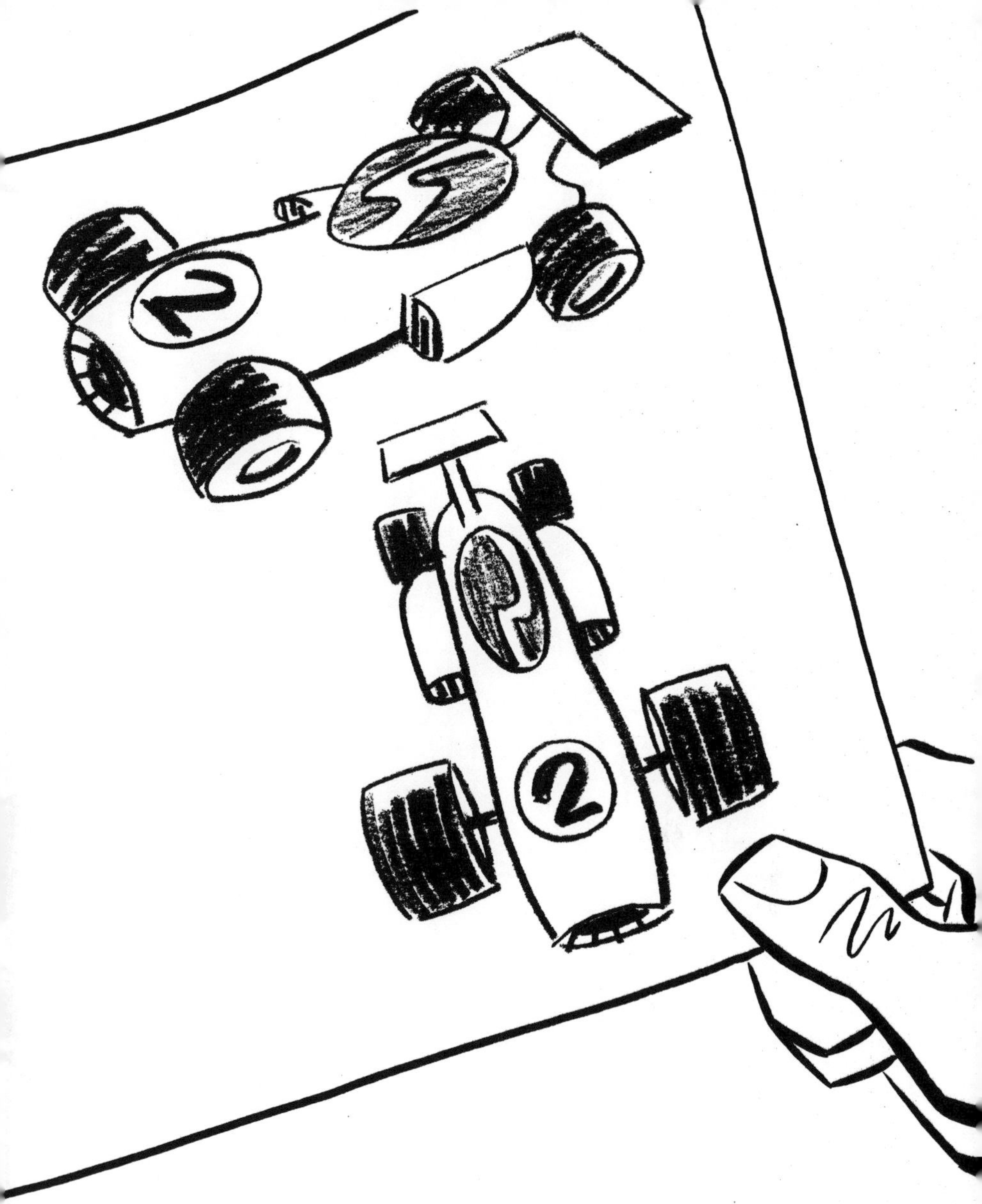

"This is *way* cooler than anything I could have dreamed up." He smiled. "Spiffier it is."

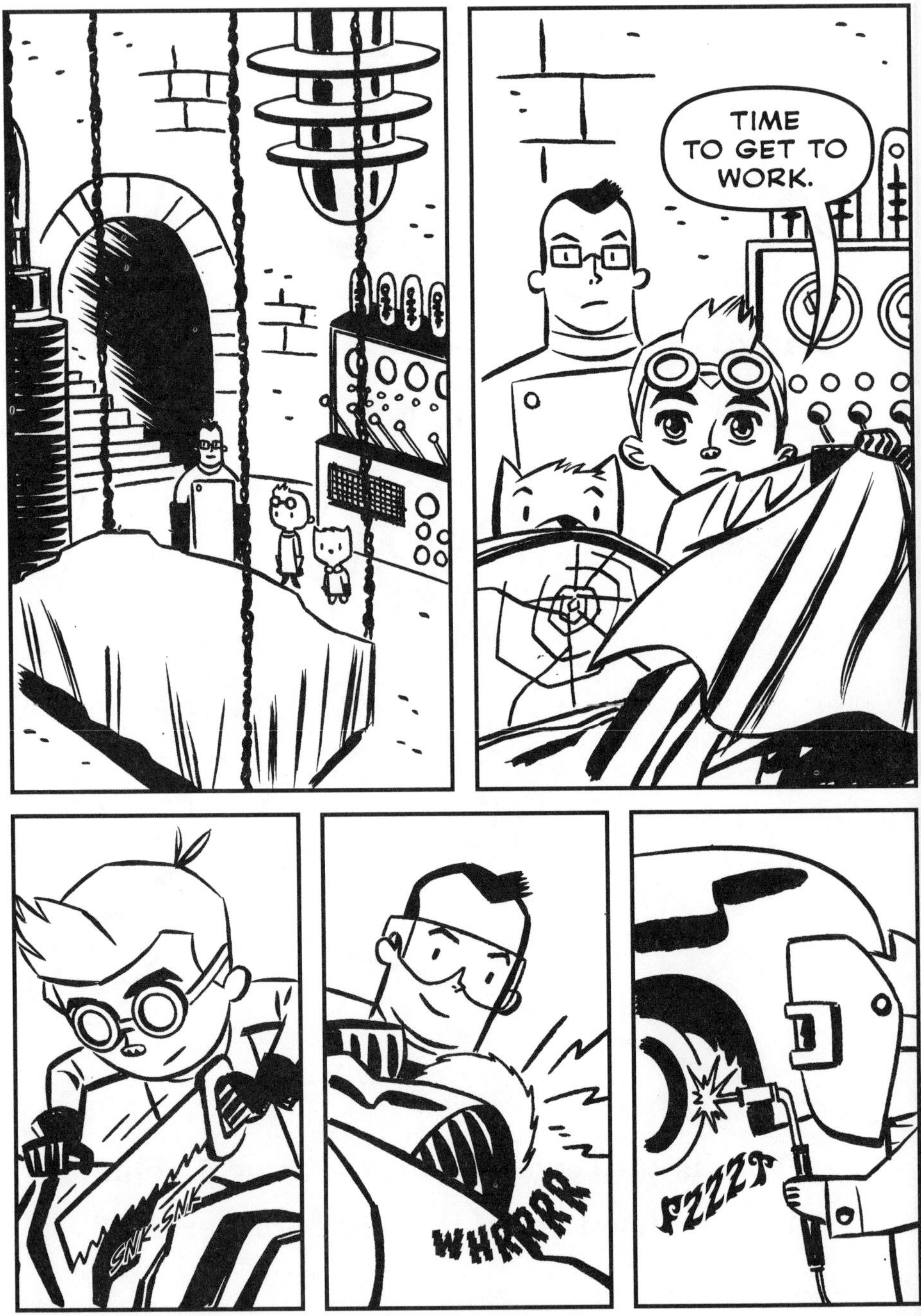
TIME TO GET TO WORK.
SNK-SNK
WHRRRR
FZZZT

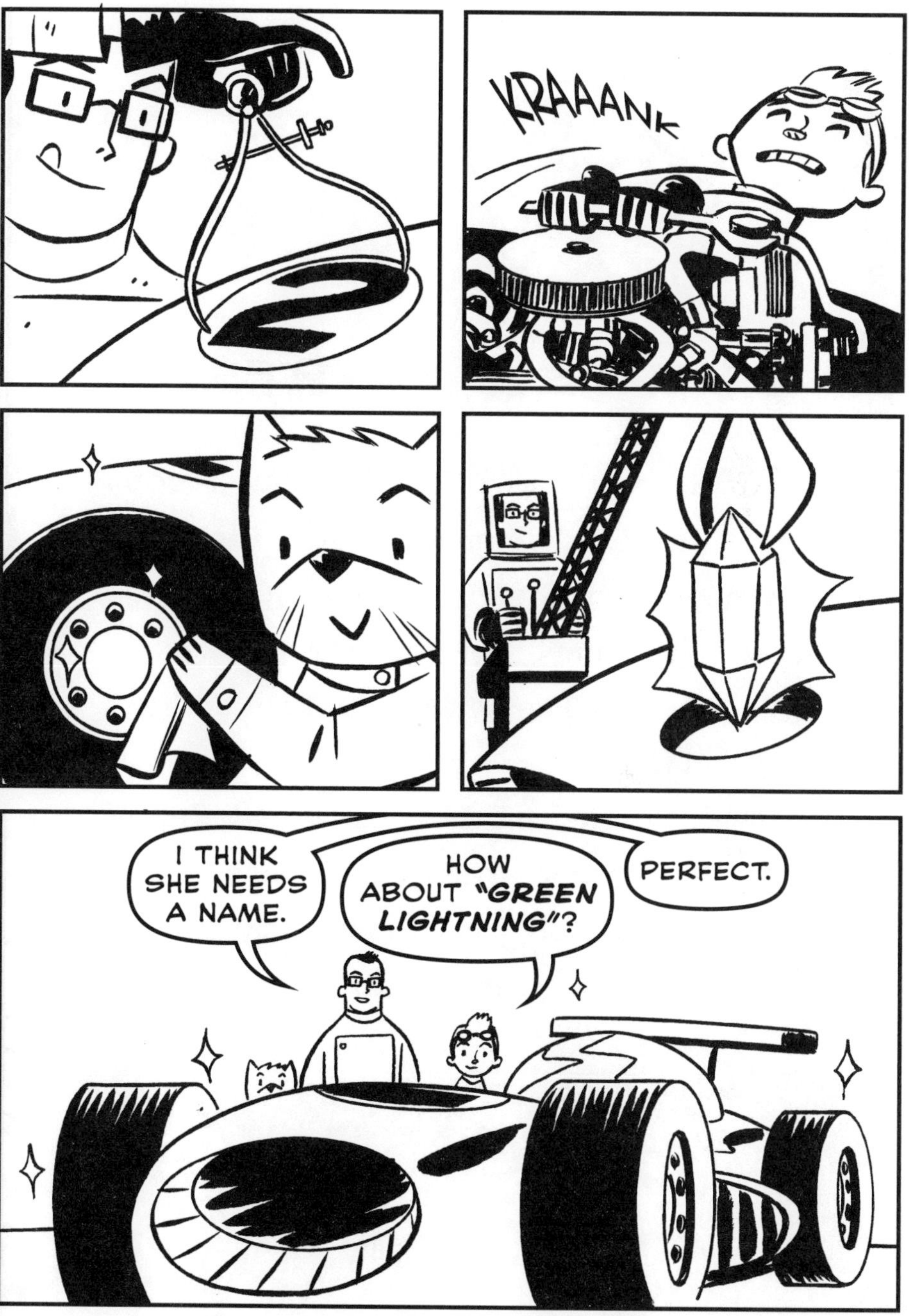
KRAAANK
I THINK SHE NEEDS A NAME.
HOW ABOUT "GREEN LIGHTNING"?
PERFECT.

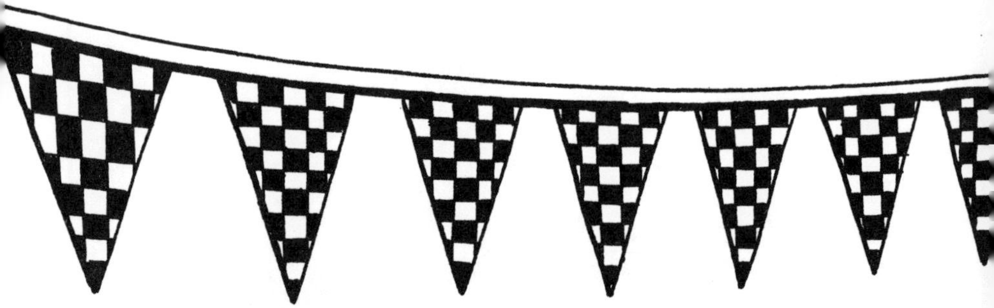

CHAPTER THIRTEEN

The big day had arrived. Scout troops were gathered from far and wide for a chance to win the Pine Run 3000. Frankie couldn't believe how packed the assembly hall was. The entire county must have been there.

From across the room, he saw Kenny. They waved their cars at each other for good luck. Kenny's car looked like a guitar with wheels.

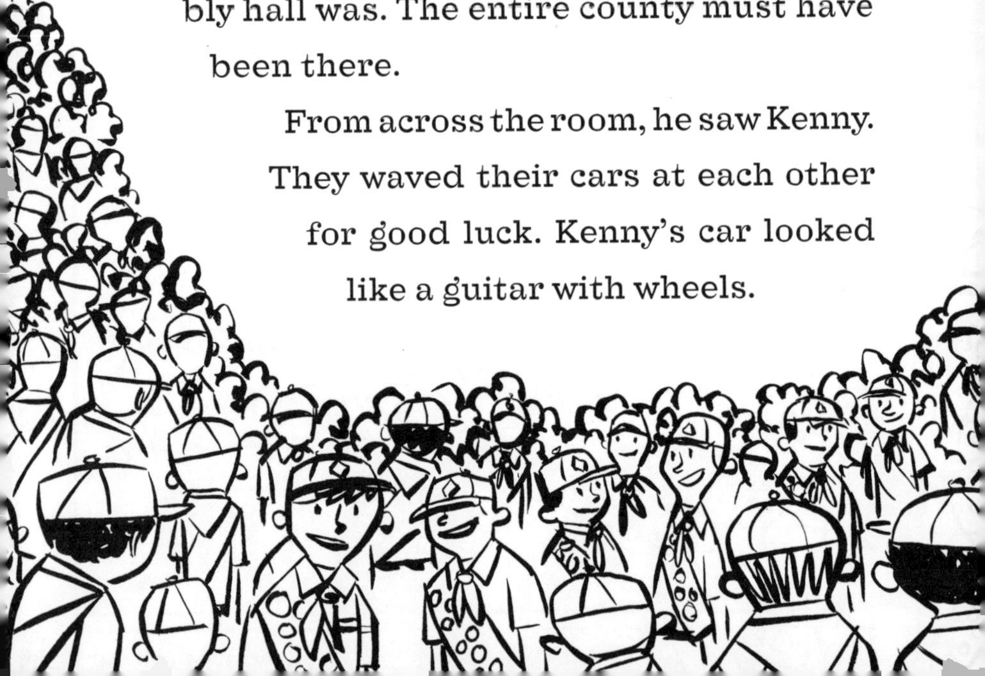

Frankie also saw the rest of his troop scattered about the crowd. He had hoped that maybe Carter would oversleep or mix up the date. But no such luck. There he was, shaking hands and posing for pictures with the Grand Possum Pooh-Bah.

Even with Green Lightning, Frankie began to worry.

Piper could see how nervous her brother was. "You don't have to beat all these kids yourself," she said. "Just stay focused on your own race, and let everyone else eliminate each other."

Piper's advice made sense. Frankie took a deep breath and felt a little calmer.

That lasted for about two seconds.

"I found your track assignment," said Dad, who had Lucy strapped to his back.

Frankie suddenly felt like he'd swallowed a swarm of butterflies.

Mom kissed him on the cheek. "Go get 'em, sweetie," she said before she had to leave to judge the races with the other Marsupial Mothers.

The race courses were divided into three areas, each with an increasing level of difficulty. Frankie's first heat was Alpine

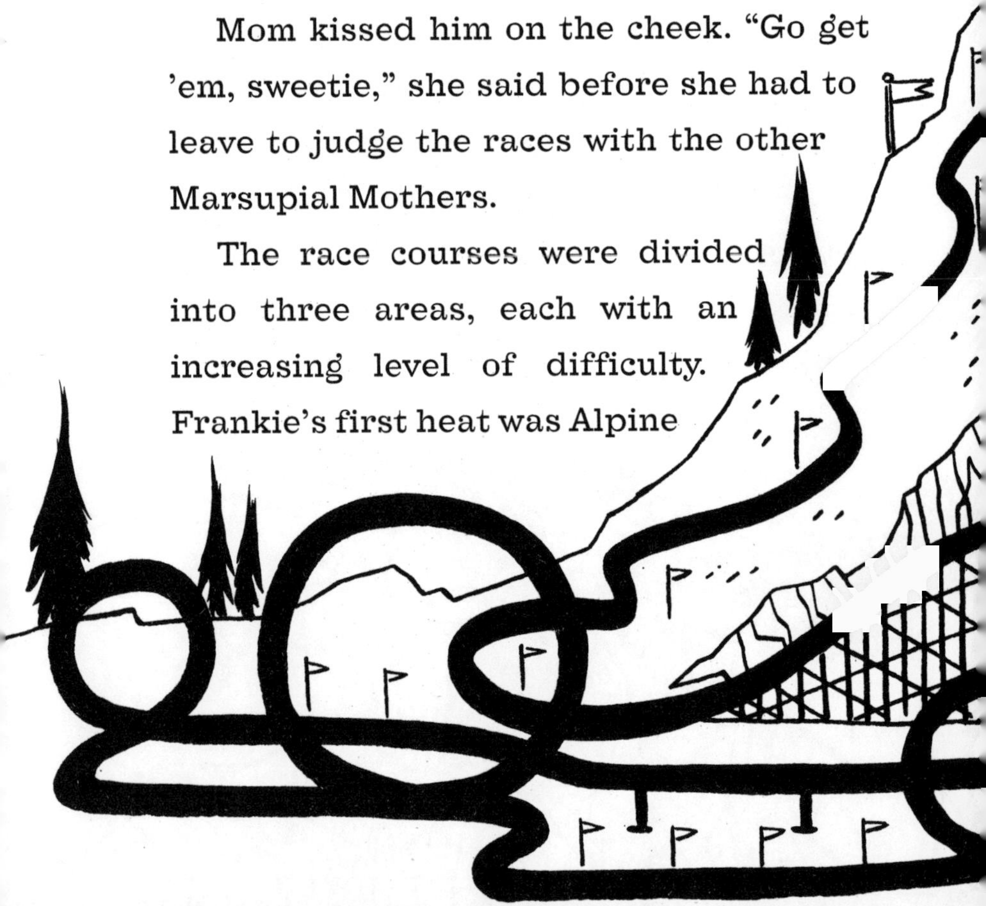

Alley. He looked across the way to his competition, but he didn't recognize any of the other seven kids. They must have been from other troops. At least he didn't have to race Carter right away. That was a relief.

Frankie placed his car on the starting line. He turned to Dad, who gave him a wink for confidence. Argyle licked his face for good luck.

Showtime.

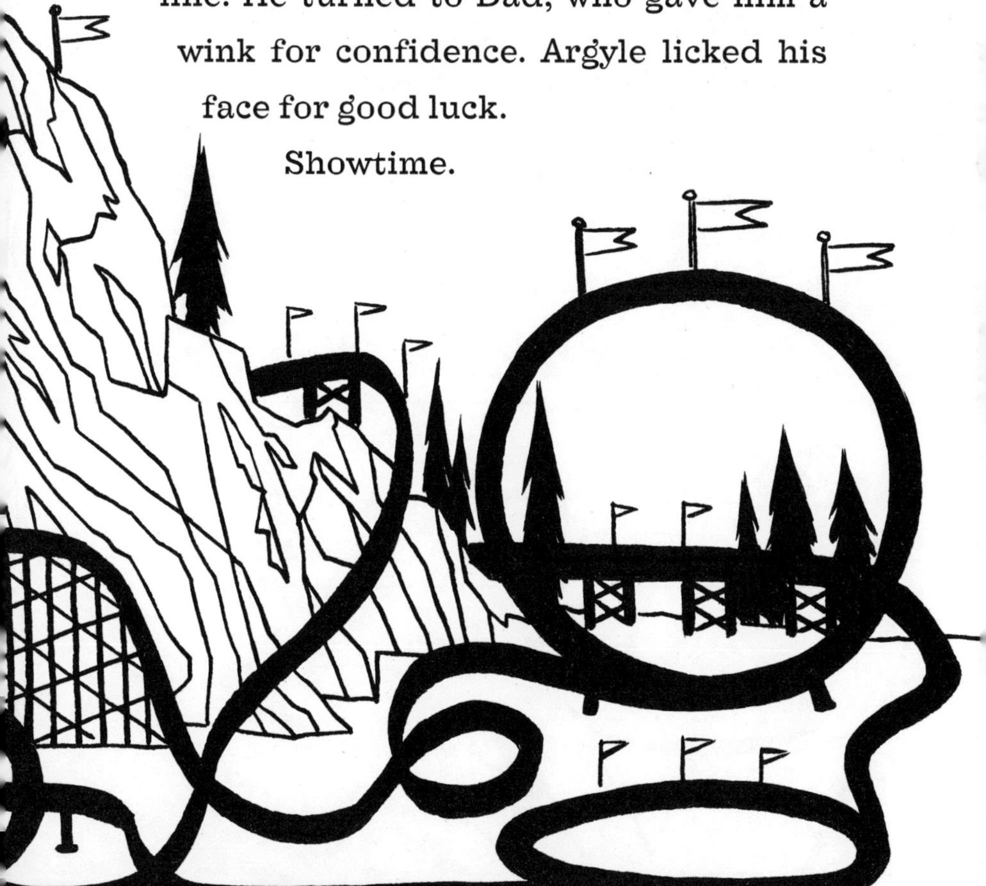

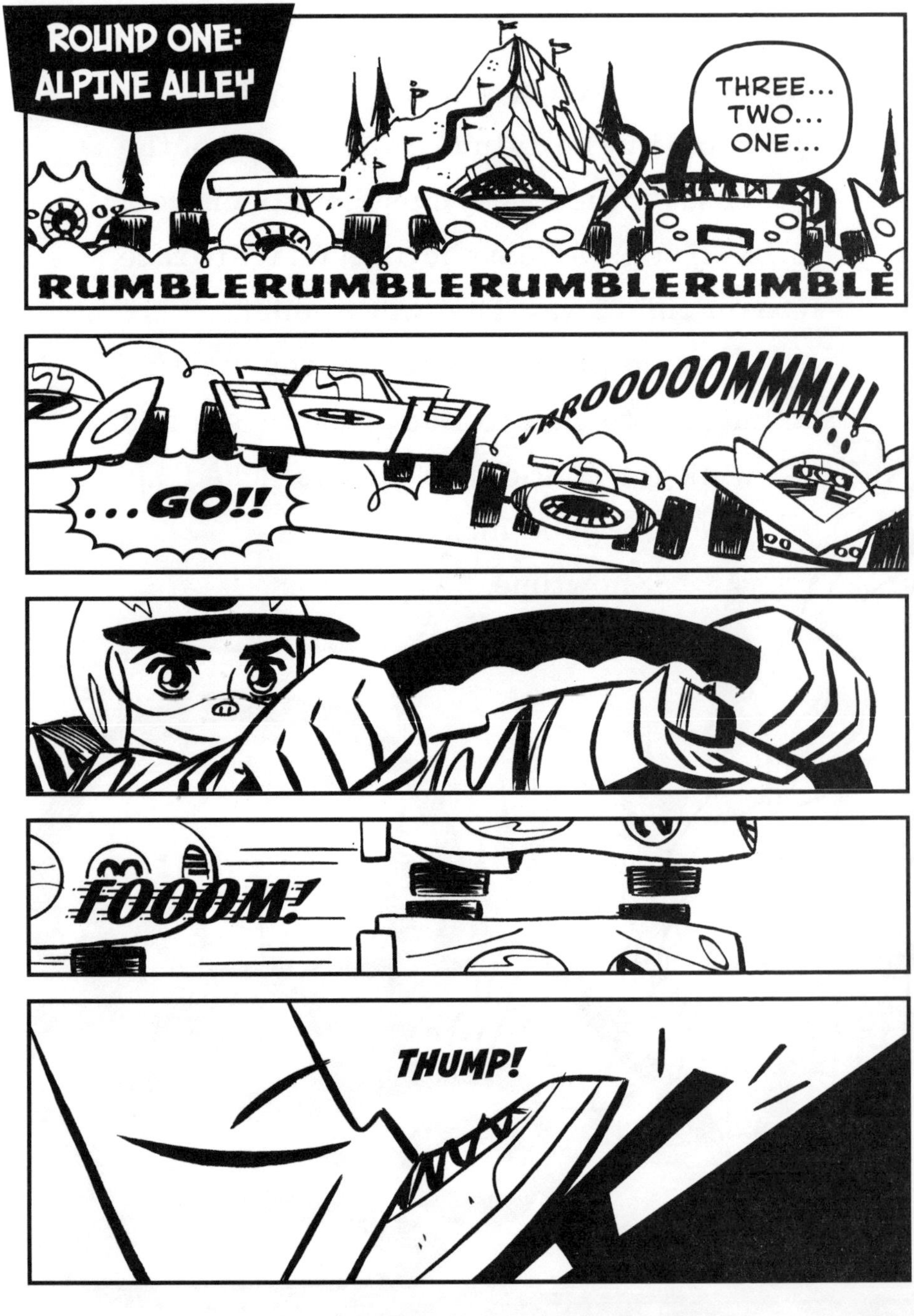

ROUND ONE:
ALPINE ALLEY
THREE...
TWO...
ONE...
RUMBLERUMBLERUMBLERUMBLE
...GO!!
VRROOOOOOMMM!!!
FOOOM!
THUMP!

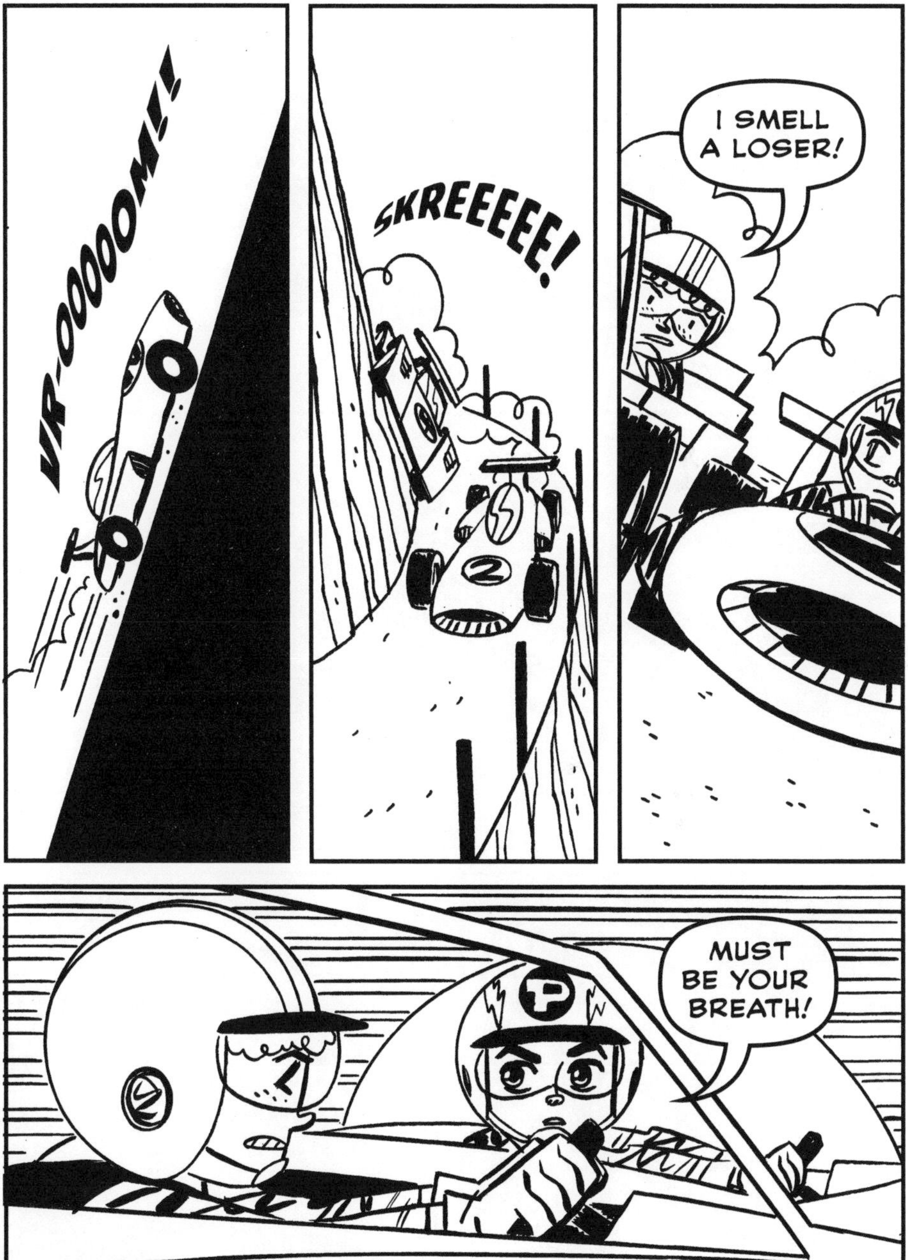
VR-OOOOOM!!
SKREEEEEE!
I SMELL A LOSER!
MUST BE YOUR BREATH!

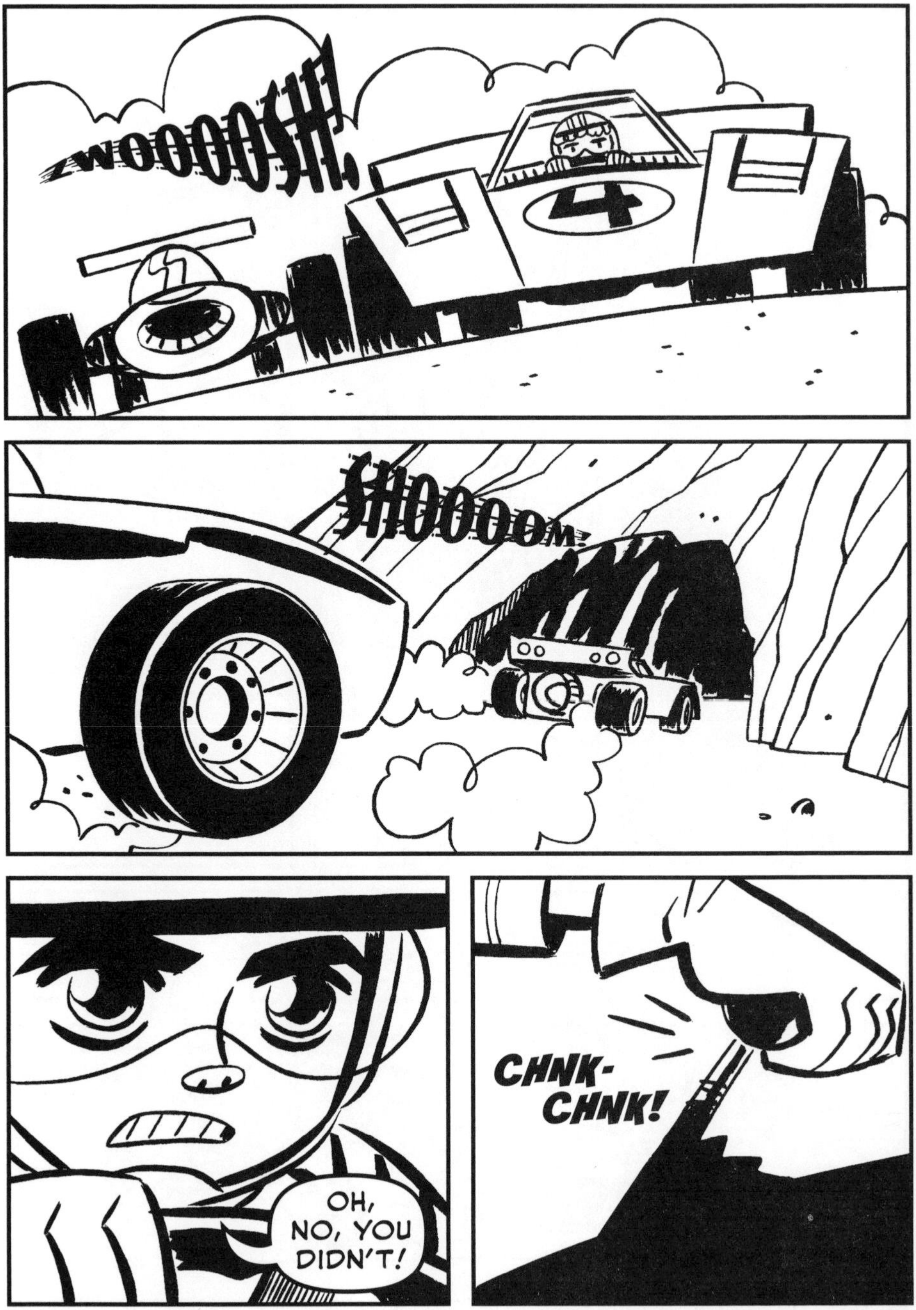
ZWOOOOSH!
SHOOOOOM!
OH, NO, YOU DIDN'T!
CHNK-CHNK!

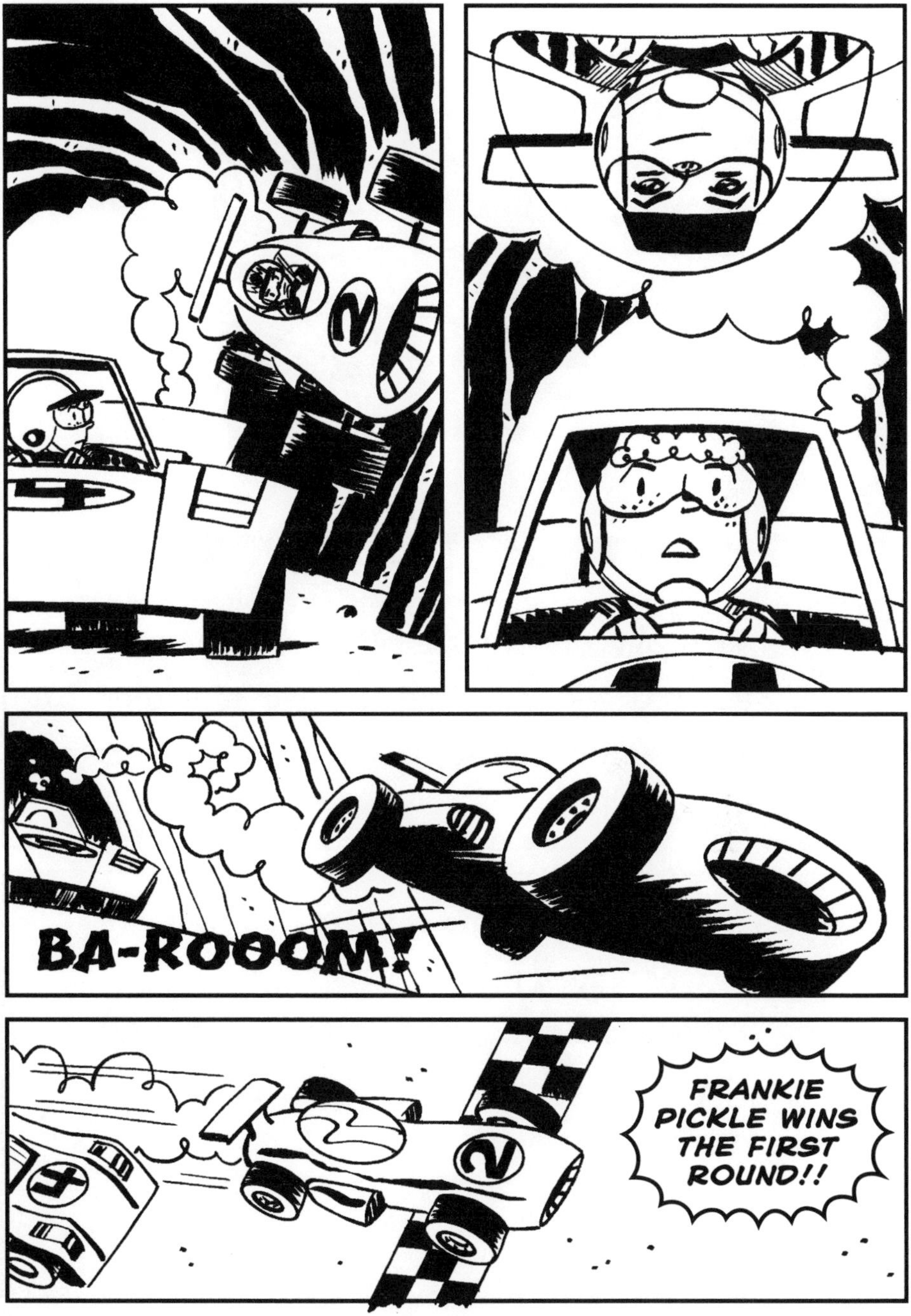
BA-ROOOM!
FRANKIE PICKLE WINS THE FIRST ROUND!!

CHAPTER FOURTEEN

Piper practically tackled Frankie, she was so excited for him. Dad hugged him too. Lucy squealed. Argyle jumped up and down on his hind legs.

Frankie couldn't believe it. He HAD won his first race! But his celebration was cut short when he saw Kenny.

"How'd it go, dude?" said Frankie. Kenny pulled out his harmonica and started playing the blues.

"Oh," said Frankie. "Sorry you didn't win."

Kenny gave a little shrug and smiled. He was happy that at least one of them was advancing. Frankie checked the standings board. Carter had won his race too.

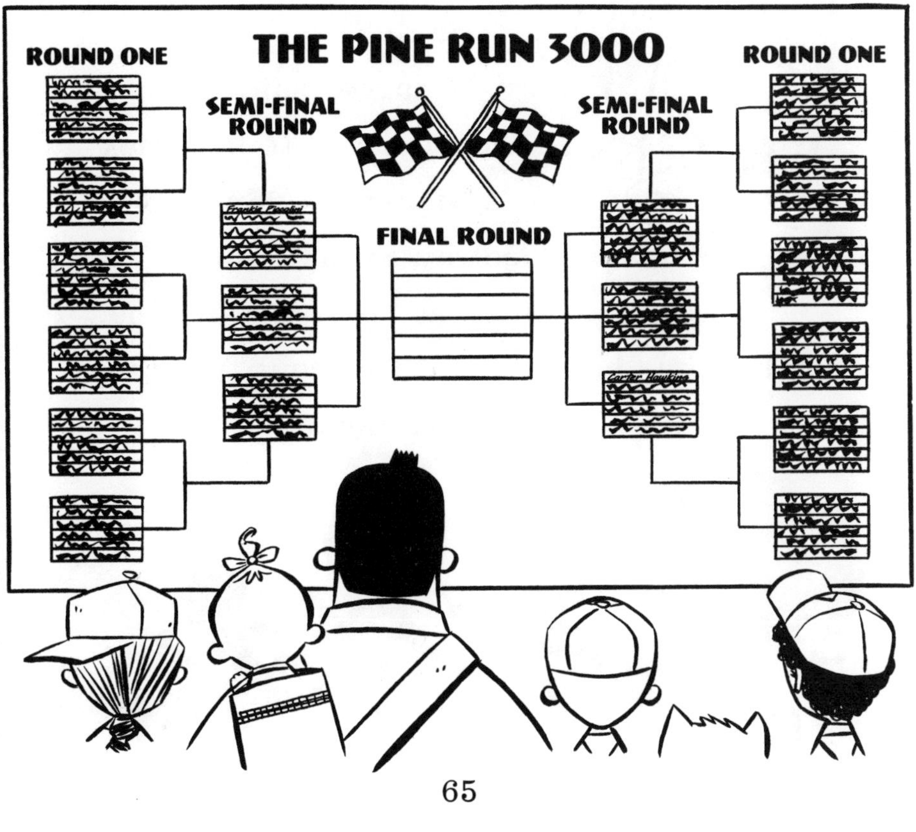
ROUND ONE
THE PINE RUN 3000
ROUND ONE
SEMI-FINAL ROUND
SEMI-FINAL ROUND
FINAL ROUND

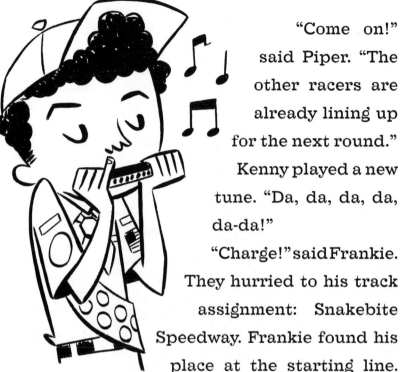

"Come on!" said Piper. "The other racers are already lining up for the next round." Kenny played a new tune. "Da, da, da, da, da-da!"

"Charge!" said Frankie. They hurried to his track assignment: Snakebite Speedway. Frankie found his place at the starting line. This time he recognized a scout from his troop. It was Melvin Grossman.

Something about Melvin never seemed quite right. Maybe it was because he liked to draw skulls on his arms with markers. Or how his laugh sounded like something out of a monster movie. Whatever it was, he gave Frankie the creeps.

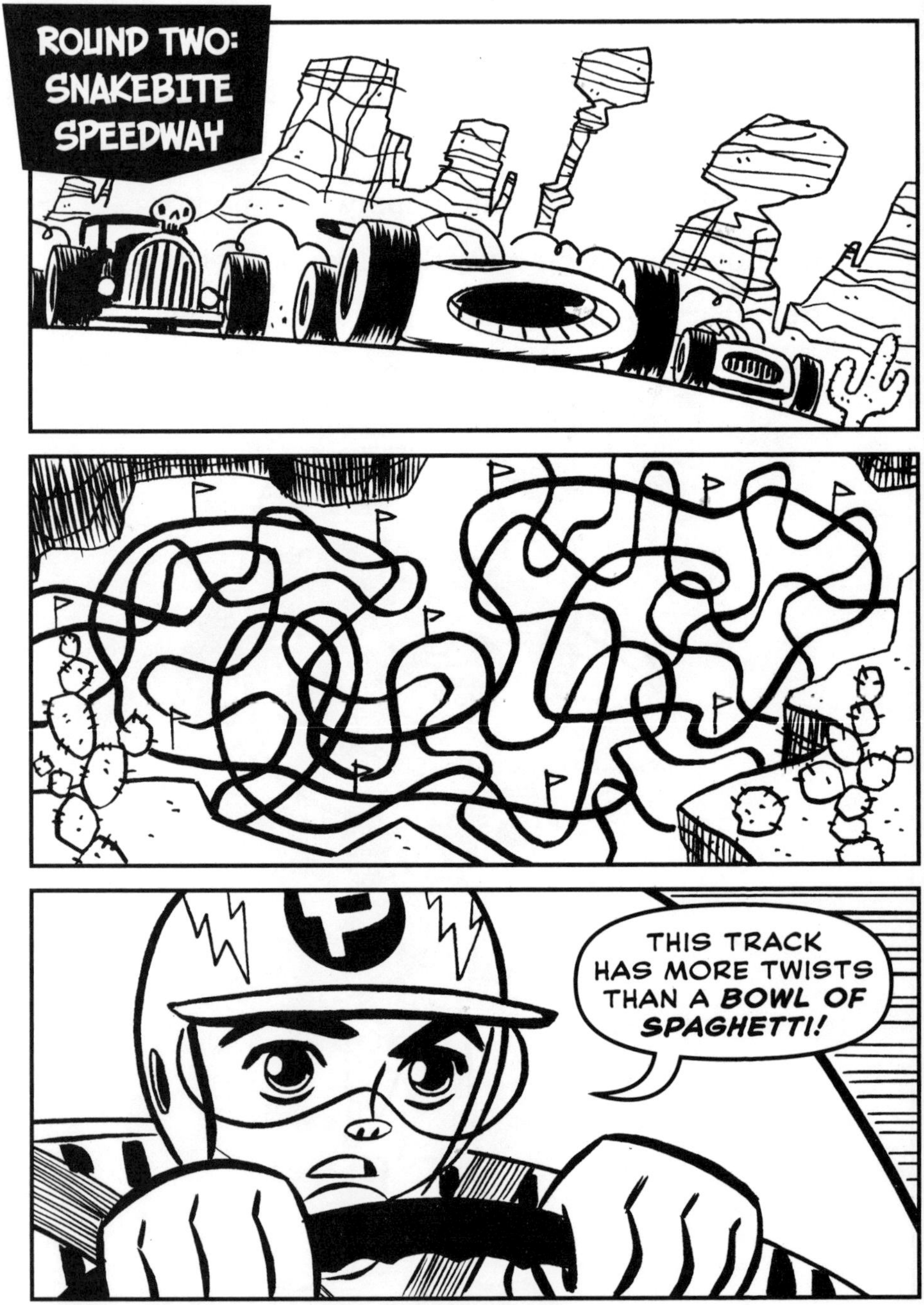
ROUND TWO: SNAKEBITE SPEEDWAY
THIS TRACK HAS MORE TWISTS THAN A *BOWL OF SPAGHETTI!*

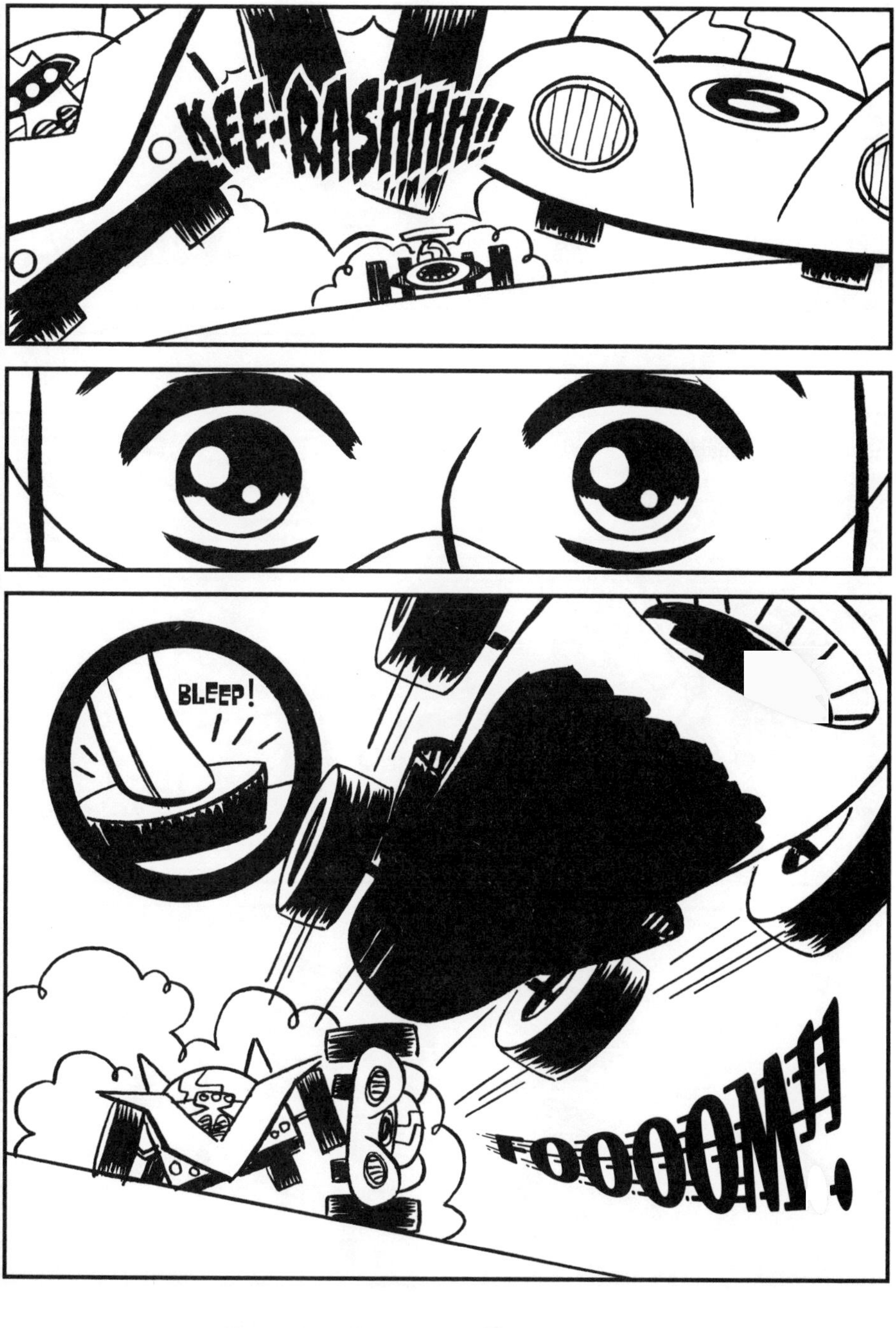
KEE-RASHHH!!
BLEEP!
FOOOOOM!!

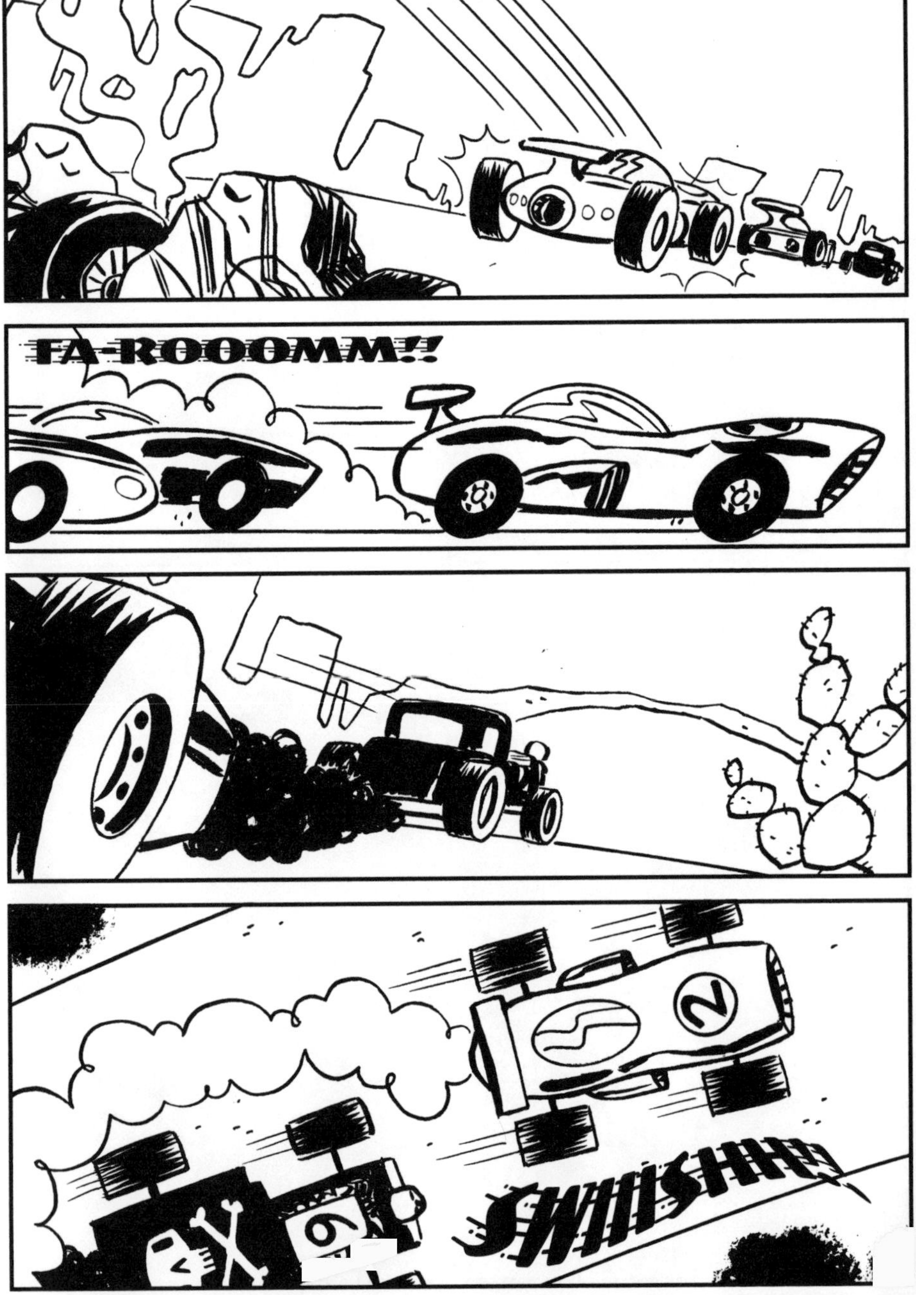
FA-ROOOOMM!!
SWIIISHH!!

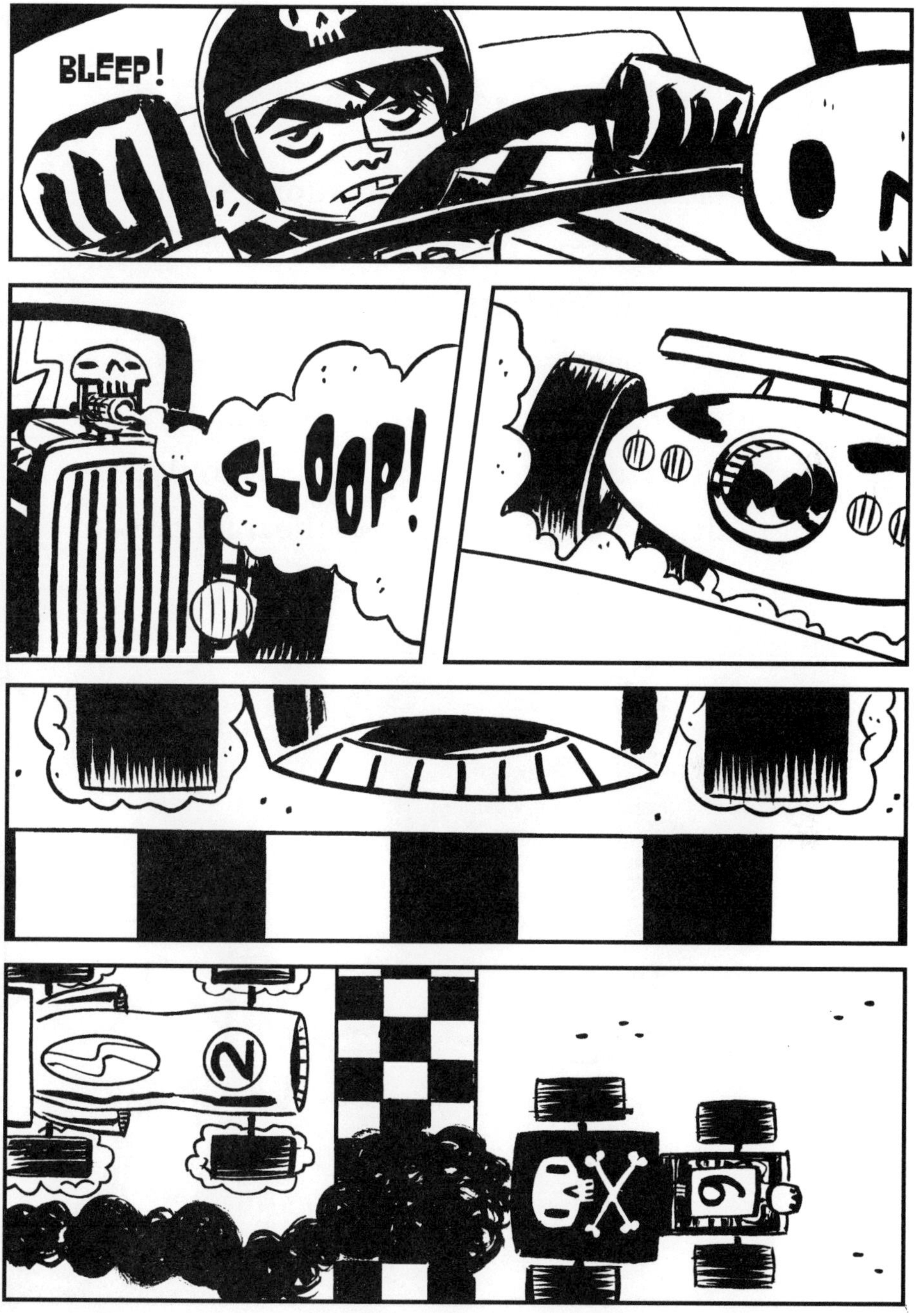
BLEEP!
GLOOP!
2
6

CHAPTER FIFTEEN

"Disqualified!" said the Marsupial Mother judging the race. "Throwing chewing gum on the track is unsportsmanlike conduct."

Melvin tried to deny he was the one who did it, but his sticky fingers gave him away. Frankie had won the semifinal round by default, and was advancing to the final race.

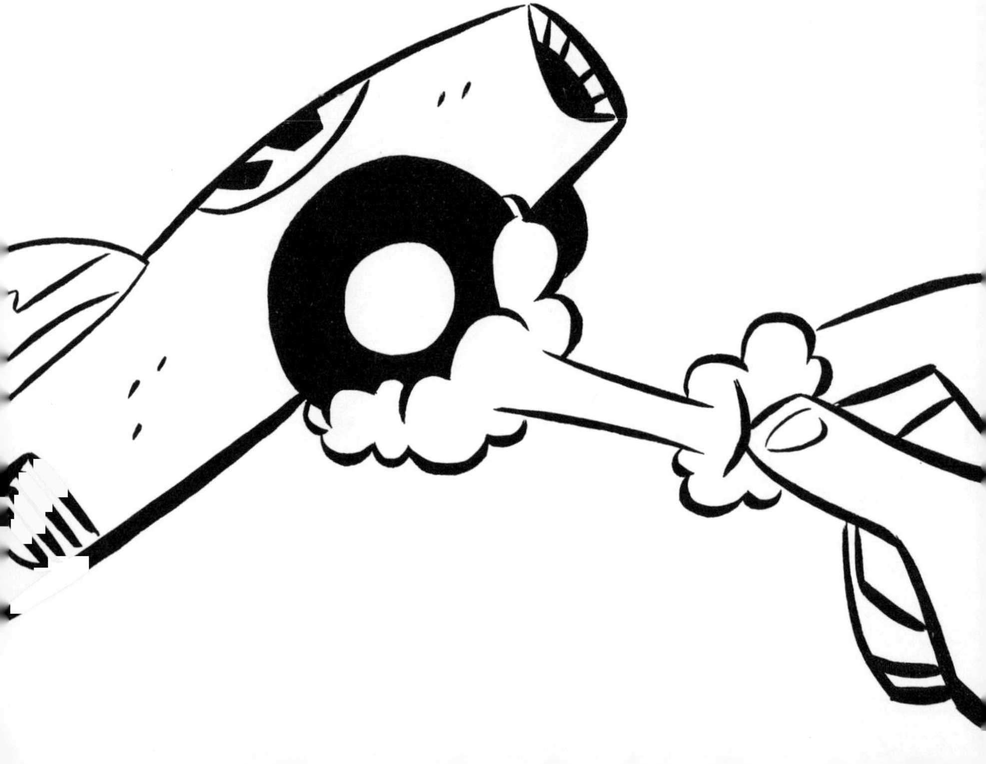

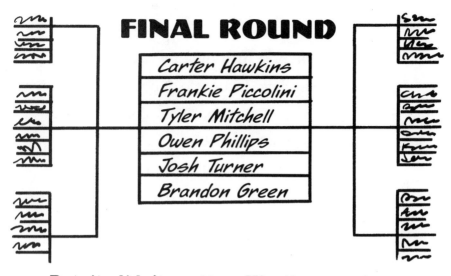

FINAL ROUND

| Carter Hawkins |
| Frankie Piccolini |
| Tyler Mitchell |
| Owen Phillips |
| Josh Turner |
| Brandon Green |

But it didn't matter. His tires were so gunked up from Melvin's gum, it would be impossible to race again. It was all over.

Carter, who had just won his race, walked over to Frankie.

"I guess you're here to rub it in," said Frankie.

"What Melvin did was really lame," said Carter. "When I beat you, Pickle, I want to win fair and square, not because he cheated."

"Well, there's no way that's going to happen. My car is ruined."

Carter reached into his emergency utility pouch and retrieved a bottle of orange liquid. He handed it to Frankie. "This goo remover should do the trick."

That was a pretty cool thing for Carter to do. Maybe he wasn't so bad after all.

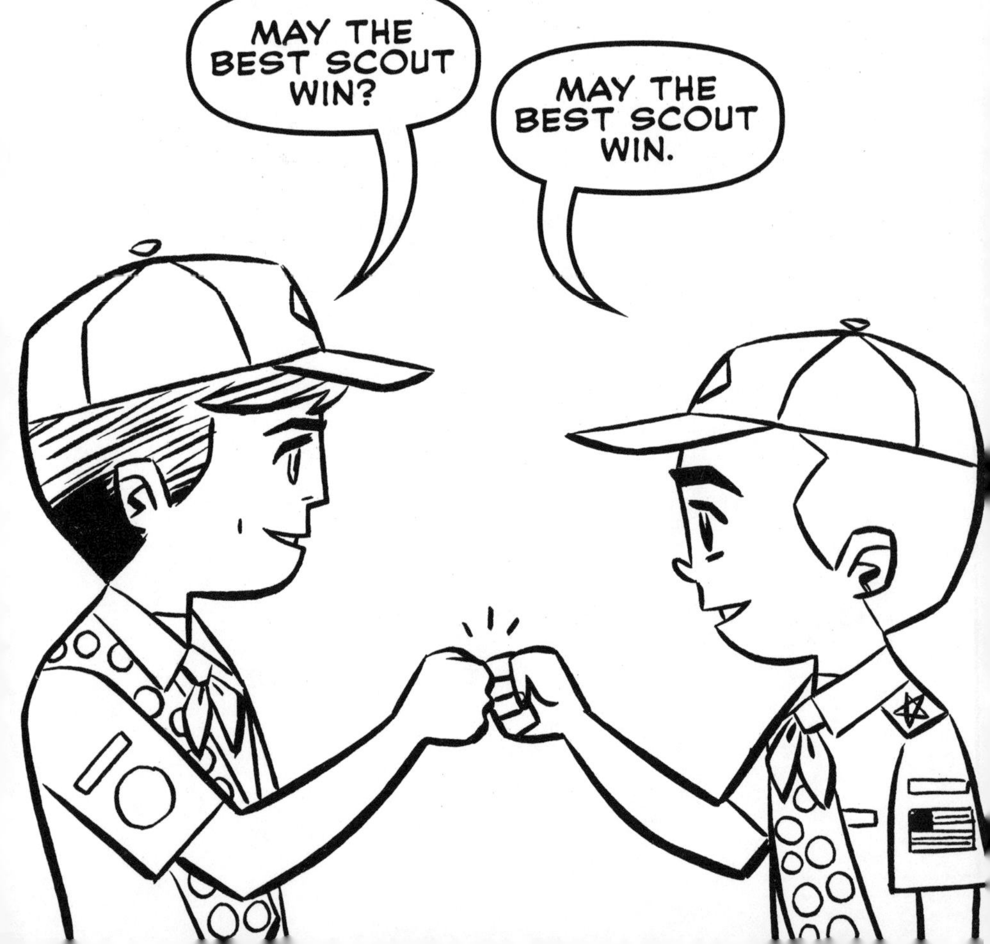
MAY THE BEST SCOUT WIN?
MAY THE BEST SCOUT WIN.

CHAPTER SIXTEEN

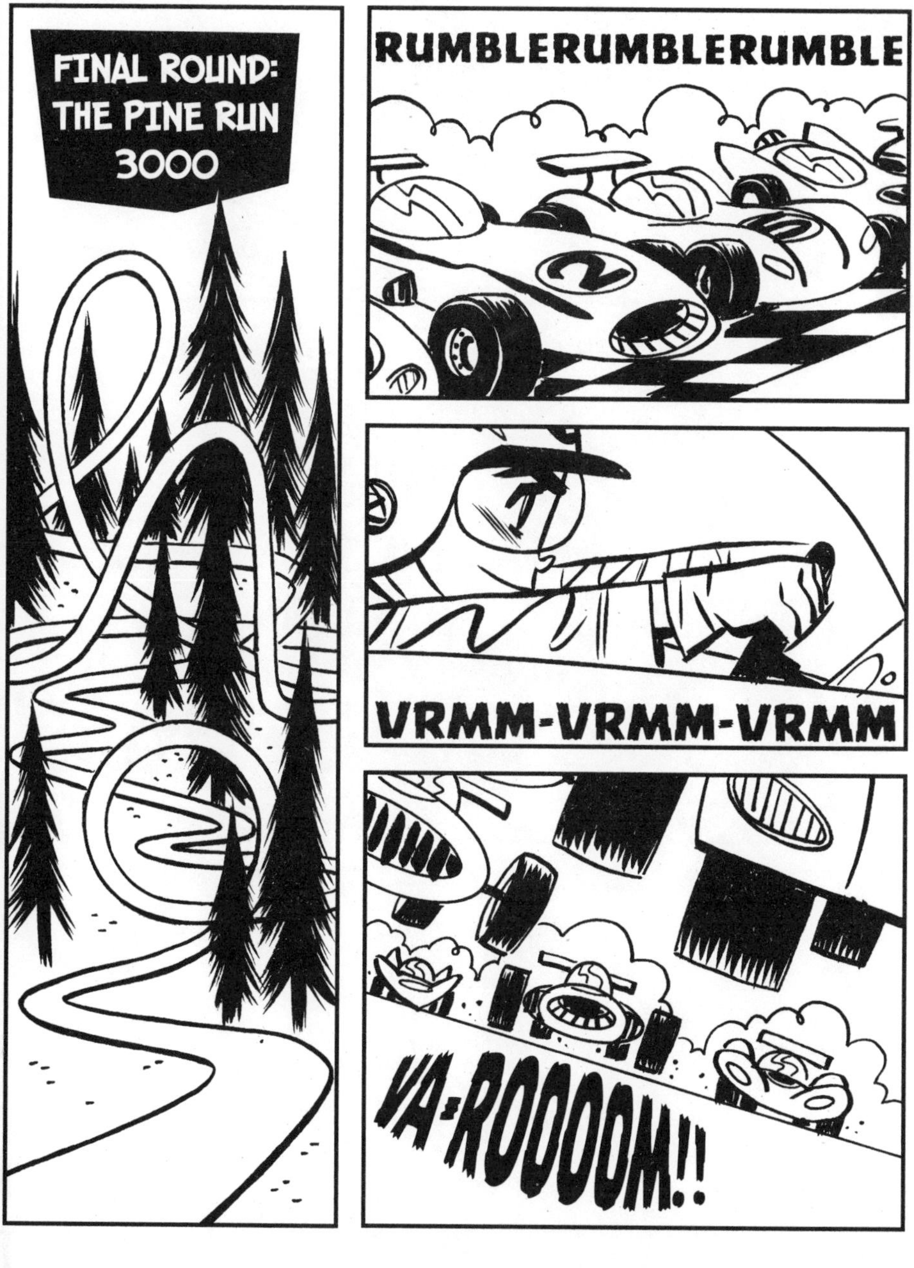
FINAL ROUND: THE PINE RUN 3000
RUMBLERUMBLERUMBLE
VRMM-VRMM-VRMM
VA-ROOOOM!!

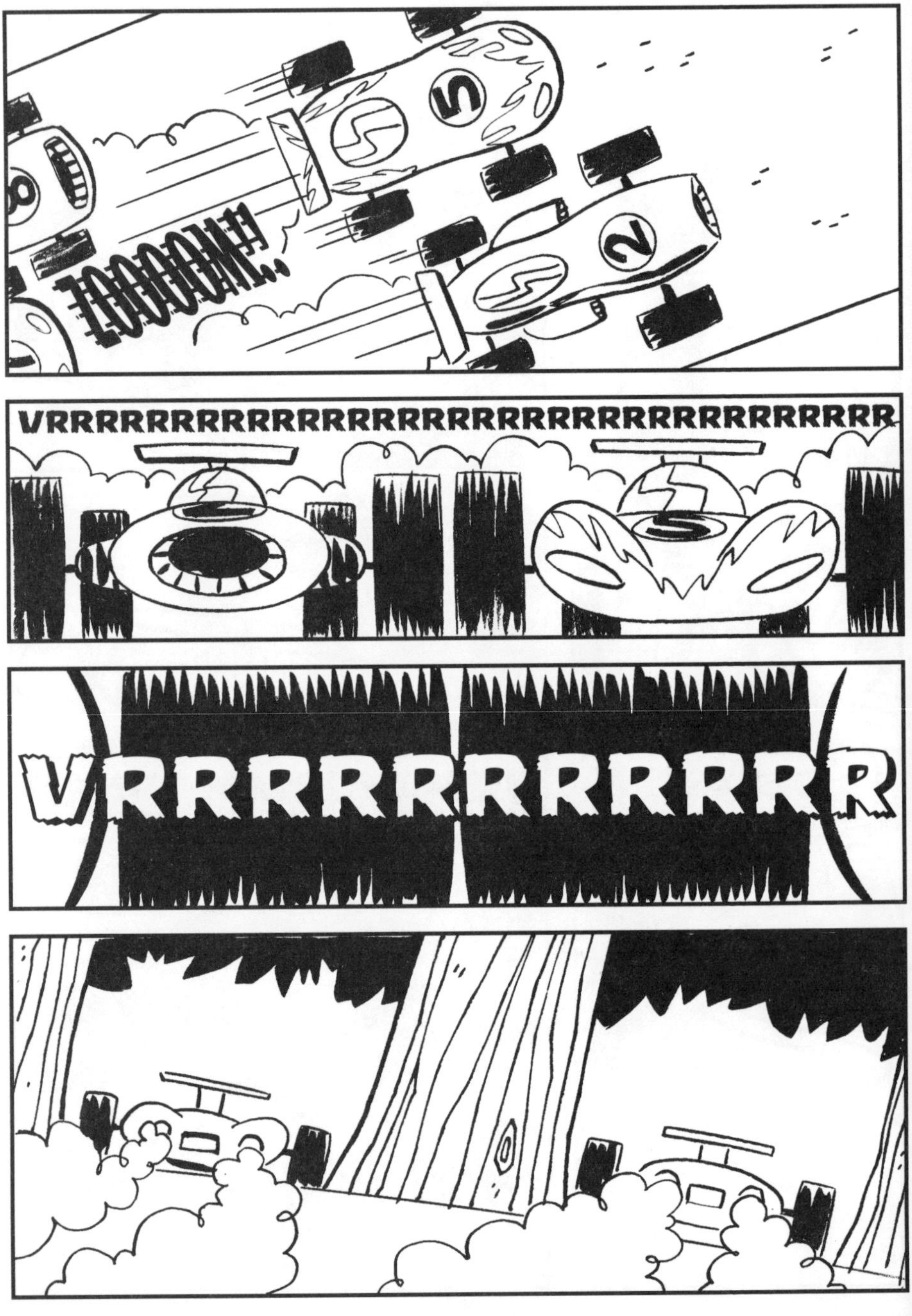
ZOOOOM!!
VRRRRRRRRRRRRRRRRRRRRRRRRRRRRRR
VRRRRRRRRRRR

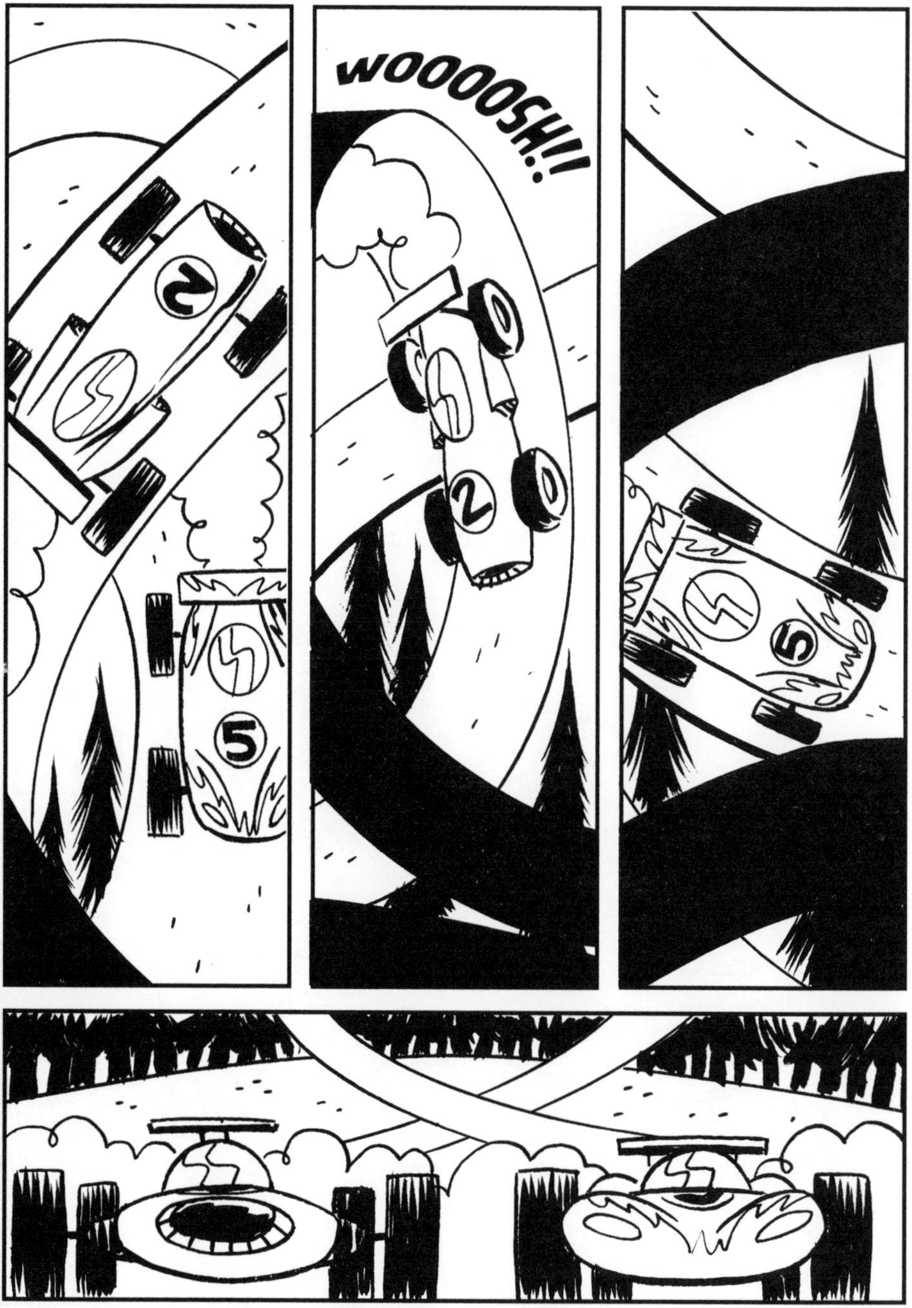
WOOOOOSH!!!

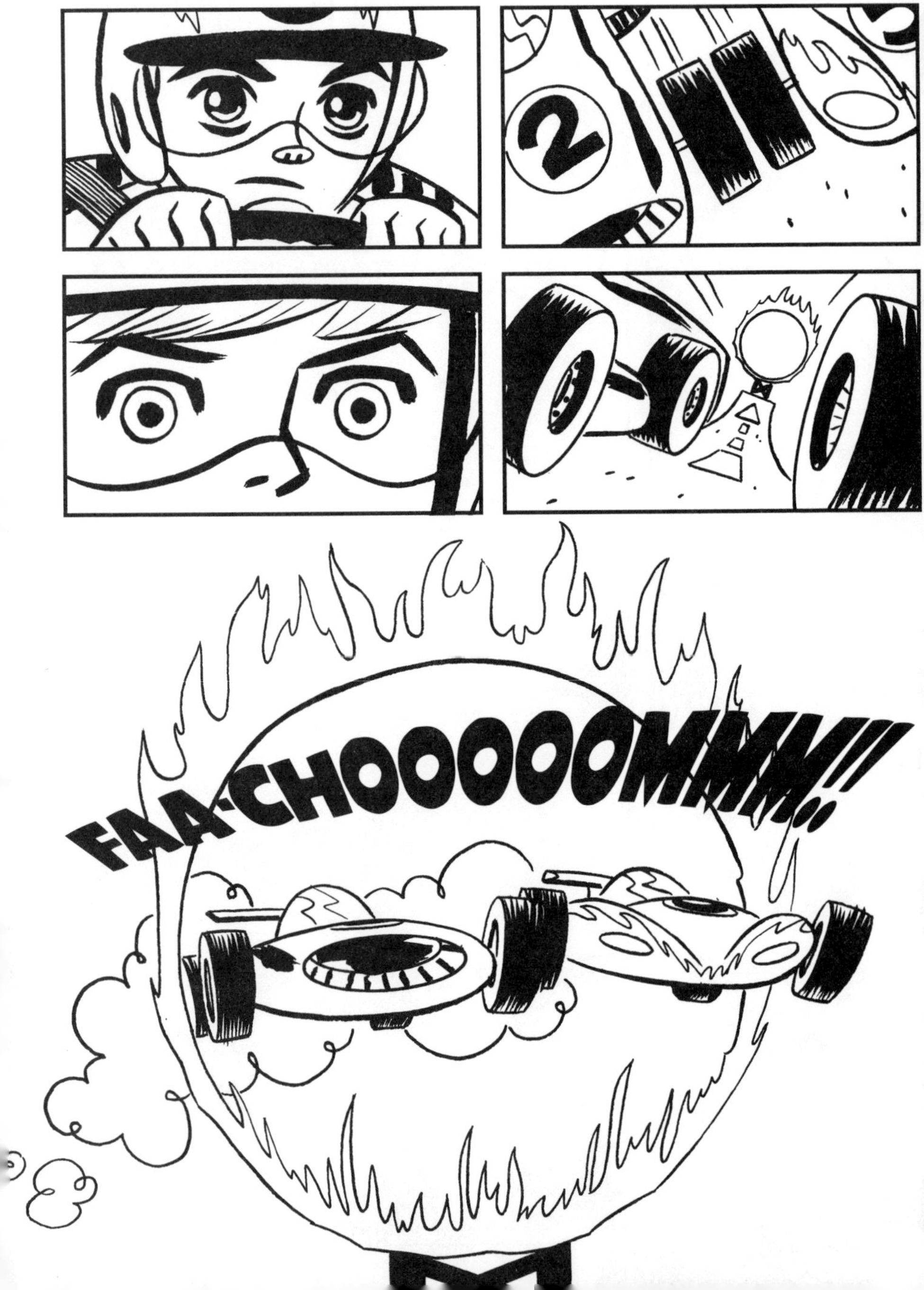
FAA-CHOOOOOOMMM!!

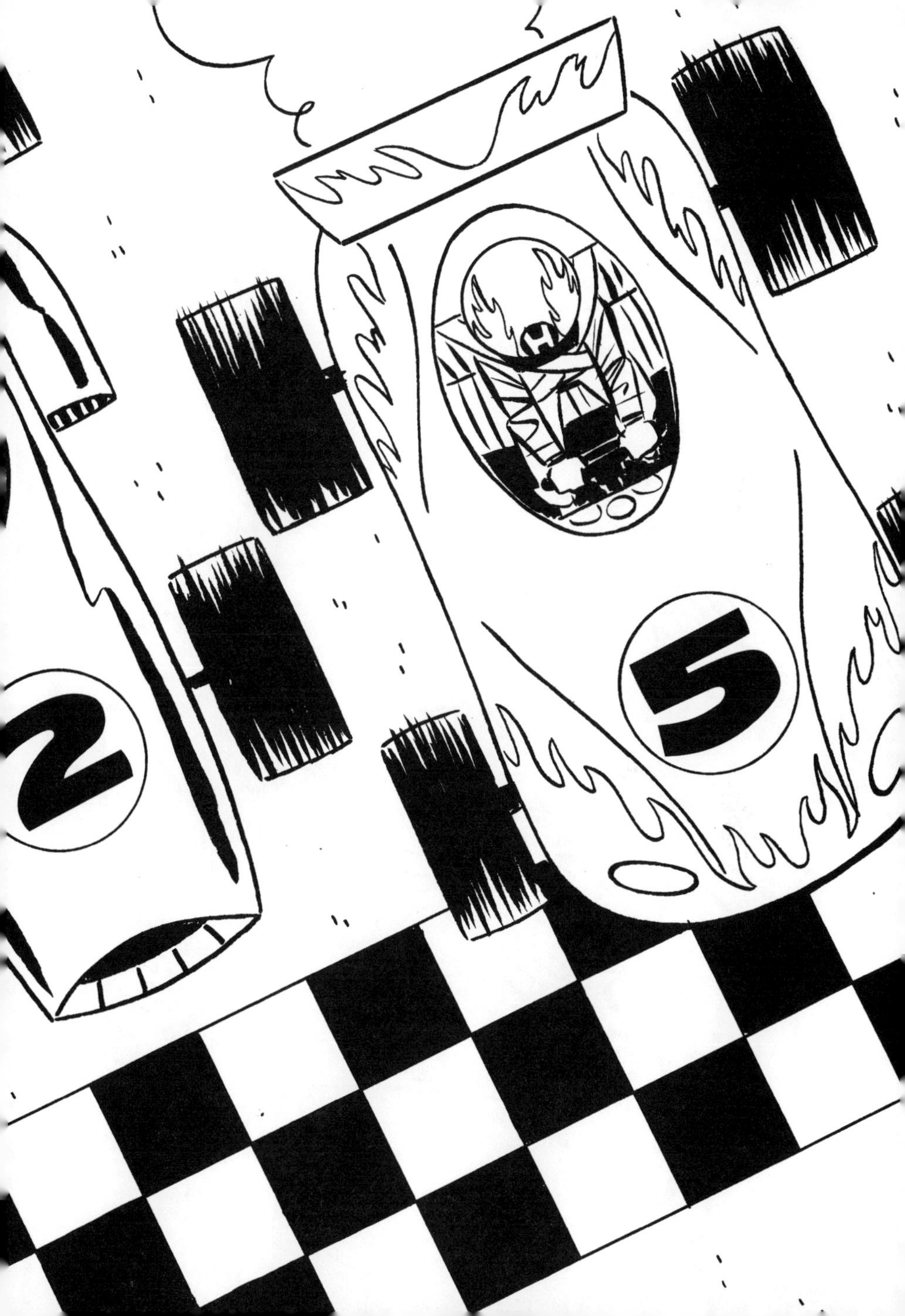

Carter Hawkins was declared the winner of the Pine Run 3000.

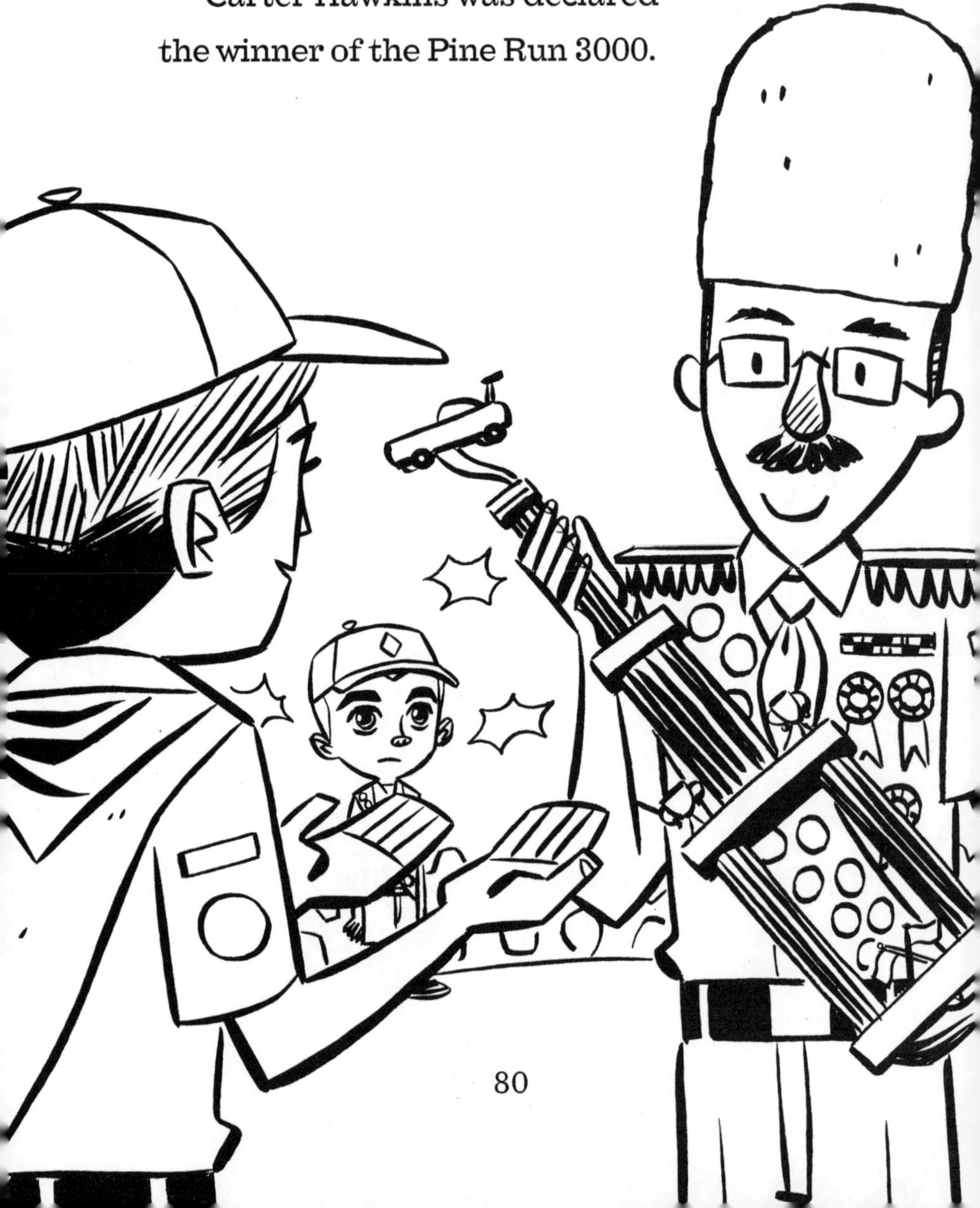

This meant that Frankie would not earn enough Possum Points to become a Shrew with the rest of his troop. He'd remain a Pygmy Possum Scout until the next session. Everyone tried to cheer Frankie up, but it was no use.

Mom and the other Marsupial Mothers stepped onto the stage with the Grand Possum Pooh-Bah to hand out the awards. The trophy for third place went to a boy from a scout troop two towns over. Frankie was called up next. He accepted his second place trophy with the biggest smile he could muster. Really, he just wanted to go home and cry. The trophy was cool, but that didn't change his rank.

Frankie held his fake smile until he was back in the crowd with his family.

"I think I'd like to go now," he said.

"Frankie, wait," said Dad.

"This isn't going to be one of those moments where you tell me winning or losing doesn't matter, is it?"

"No, I was going to tell you that they haven't announced all the winners yet."

"Huh?"

The Grand Possum Pooh-Bah's voice boomed through the hall. "Franklin Lorenzo Piccolini!"

Everybody was applauding. Argyle howled. Kenny whistled the loudest.

Dad gave Frankie a little nudge toward the stage and said, "Don't keep the Grand Possum Pooh-Bah waiting."

CHAPTER SEVENTEEN

Frankie slowly made his way to the front of the crowd. It all felt like a dream. Strangers ruffled his hair and patted him on the back and gave him high fives. Even Carter was cheering for him.

"Looks like we're both winners, dude!" said Carter.

Standing on the stage next to the Grand Possum Pooh-Bah was Mom, all smiles and tears. She was holding a medal that looked different from the other awards.

"Congratulations, Frankie," said the

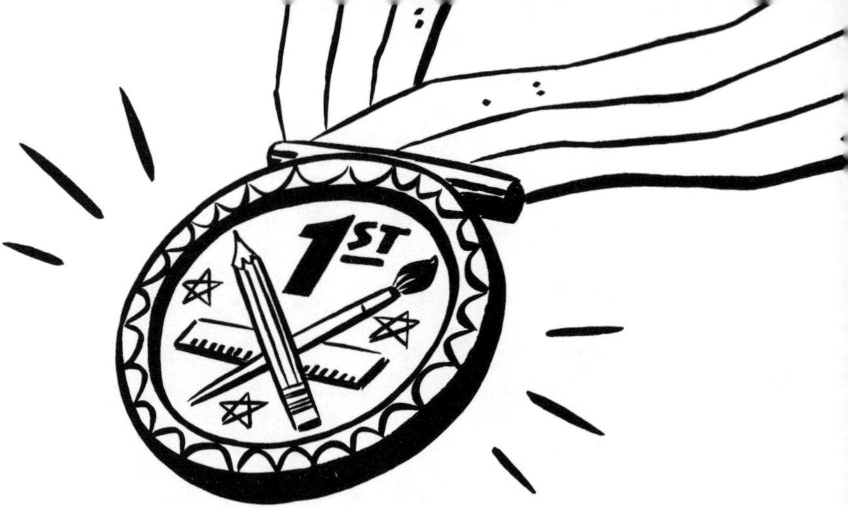
1ST

Grand Possum Pooh-Bah as he shook Frankie's hand.

"I don't understand," said Frankie.

"You won first place for Most Outstanding Race-Car Design," said the Grand Possum Pooh-Bah.

Frankie had been so upset about losing to Carter, he didn't even realize there were any other prizes.

"Does this mean I have enough Awesome, I mean, Possum Points to become a Shrew Scout?"

"Yes, it does," said Mom.

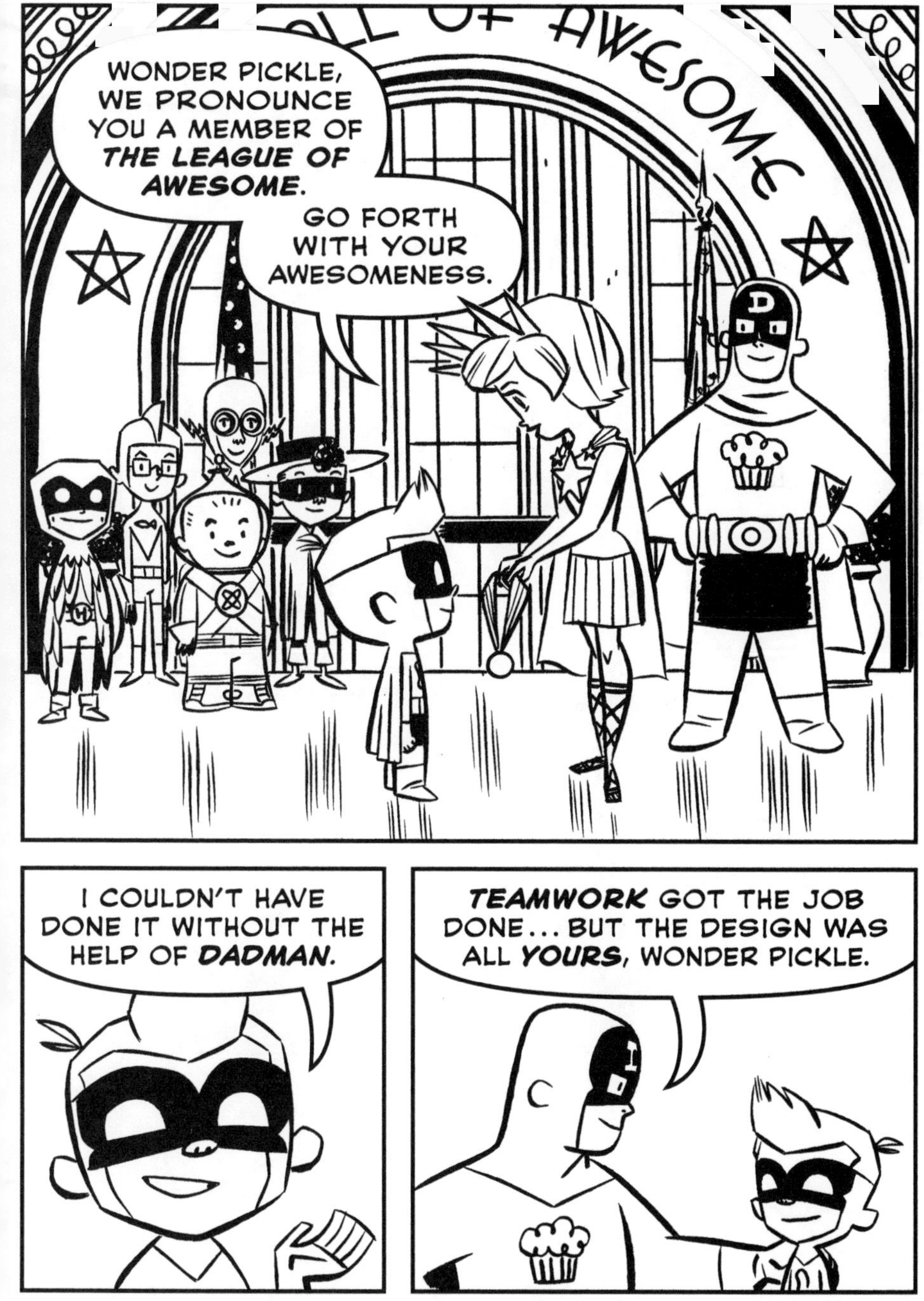

LL OF AWESOME
WONDER PICKLE, WE PRONOUNCE YOU A MEMBER OF ***THE LEAGUE OF AWESOME***.
GO FORTH WITH YOUR AWESOMENESS.
I COULDN'T HAVE DONE IT WITHOUT THE HELP OF ***DADMAN***.
TEAMWORK GOT THE JOB DONE... BUT THE DESIGN WAS ALL ***YOURS***, WONDER PICKLE.

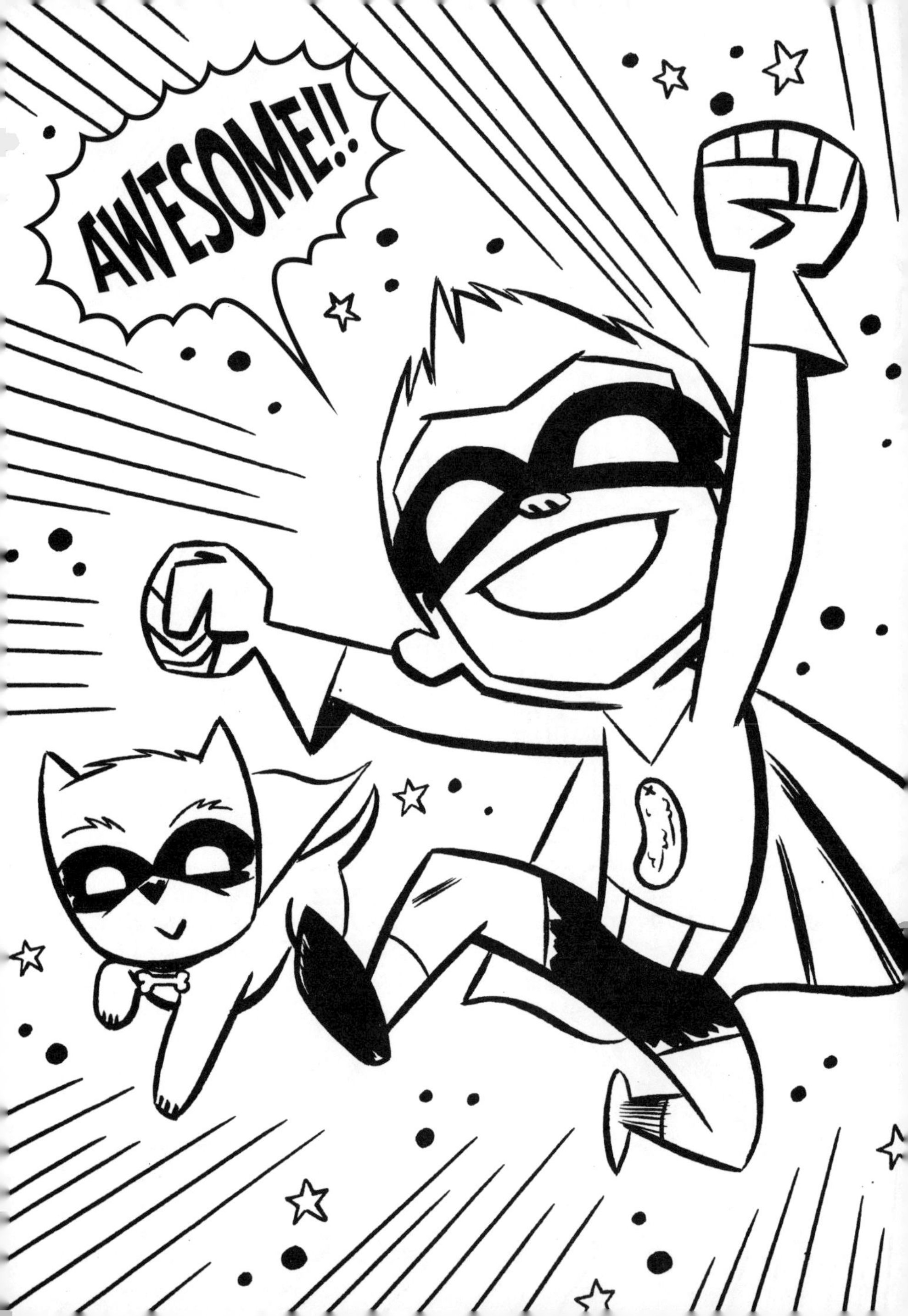
AWESOME!!

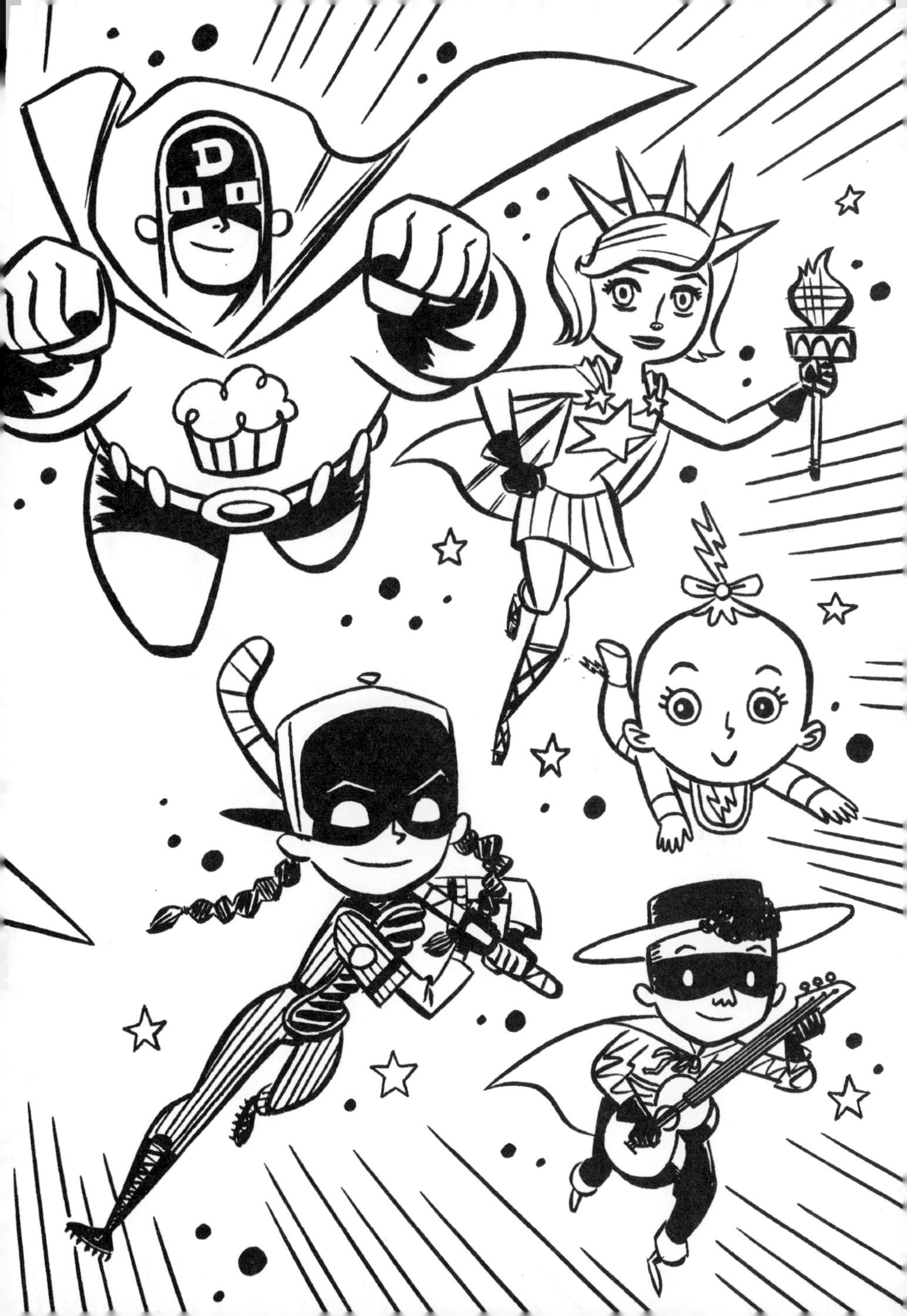

ABOUT THE CREATOR

Eric Wight spent his childhood wishing for superpowers. When that didn't pan out, he decided to learn how to write and draw. And while he may never fly or shoot lasers from his fingertips, getting to tell stories and make people laugh for a living is pretty cool too.

Maybe his wish came true after all.

Check out all the fun he's having at
ericwight.com.

ARM YOURSELF AND ADD FRANKIE'S NEXT ADVENTURE TO YOUR COLLECTION!

FRANKIE PICKLE™ AND THE MATHEMATICAL MENACE

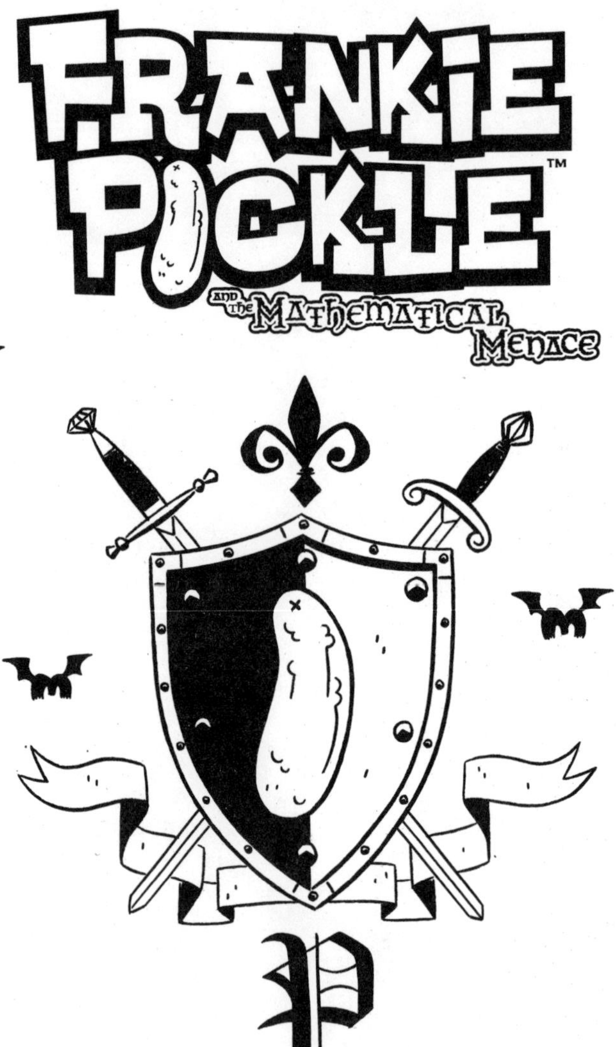

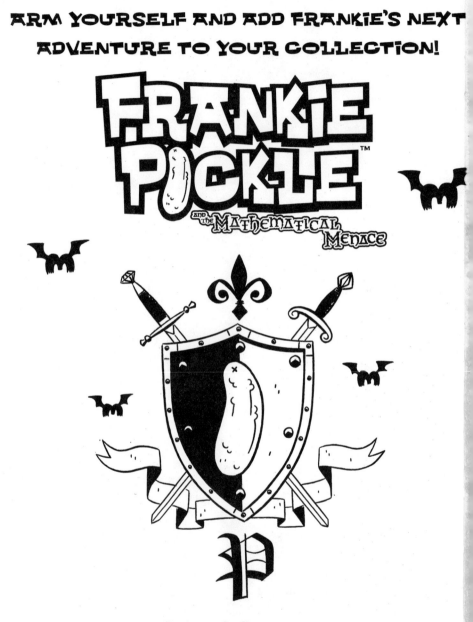

SIMON & SCHUSTER
BOOKS FOR YOUNG READERS